# THE DRE

Judy Allen has worked in the theatre, in a literary agency and in publishing. But for several years she has been a full-time writer, and now has over twenty books – some fiction, some non-fiction – to her name. Her novels for young people include *Travelling Hopefully*, *Something Rare and Special* and *Awaiting Developments*, which won the Whitbread Award and the Friends of the Earth Earthworm Award, as well as being commended for the Carnegie medal. She has also written some City Farm stories for younger children and two adult novels, the first of which, *December Flower*, was made into a television film.

Judy Allen rarely, if ever, gets a complete idea for a book at once. "Usually there are bits and pieces of ideas drifting around," she says, "and then one last, perhaps quite small thing will come along and I'll see how they link together into one book. Even when that happens, I can't begin until I've thought a lot about the main characters so that I feel I know them." One of the main "characters" in all her books is the place where the book is set – as in *The Dream Thing*, where a piece of wasteground by a flyover assumes a menacing significance to the central character, Jen, when gypsies set up camp there.

Judy Allen lives in Putney, London.

Also by Judy Allen

For Younger Readers

*The Dim Thin Ducks*
*The Great Pig Sprint*

For Older Readers

*Awaiting Developments*
*Something Rare and Special*
*Travelling Hopefully*

# THE DREAM THING

## JUDY ALLEN

00034

WALKER BOOKS
LONDON

The book Tom reads from on pages 35 and 36 is
*Touch the Earth*, compiled by T. C. McLuhan,
published by the Garnstone Press, 1972.

First published 1978 by Hamish Hamilton Children's Books
This edition published 1991 by Walker Books Ltd
87 Vauxhall Walk, London SE11 5HJ

© 1978 Judy Allen
Cover illustration © 1990 Richard Parent

Printed and bound in Great Britain by
Cox and Wyman Ltd, Reading, Berkshire

British Library Cataloguing in Publication Data
A catalogue record is available for this book
from the British Library
ISBN 0-7445-2058-4

# 1

WRITE AN ESSAY, was the instruction, about what matters most to you. Of all the apparently impossible subjects they'd ever been given, that seemed to Jen to be the first totally impossible one.

The thing that matters most to me is hate.

That would make them angry. They would think it was said for effect. Even if you knew that hate mattered most to you in the sense that it had the strongest effect on your life, carried the greatest power to motivate, to change; even if you knew that it mattered because you knew it could get away from you, and form a life of its own, and control your whole mind, you couldn't say so without provoking silly comments.

And there were enough silly comments at school at the moment without provoking them from the staff. Even Tom had been stupid lately, never actually saying anything unkind himself, but laughing at her when she reacted to the others. It was probably only a phase, like skateboarding had been a phase, and smoking, and shoplifting from Woolworths. But it seemed to Jen to be more robust than any of the other phases.

"Hallo gypsy," they said.

"Did your mother run away with the tinkers, then?"

"Whose mother was a naughty girl?"

And sang the song about the raggle-taggle gypsies that was still in the school song book, just as it had been in her mother's day and, presumably, her grandmother's day.

They were energetic but unoriginal, and they made her too angry to hide her feelings. Then they mimicked the way she banged her books about, frowned, flared her nostrils. . . . "The wind'll change," they said. They got confused and called her a changeling—or they asked her to tell their fortunes, which was something she wouldn't try for fear of finding she could do it.

She was never quite clear in her mind whether it was her mother not being married or her father having been a gypsy that got up their noses. And so the two became fused in her mind into one big, angry shame that seemed to shine on her like a spotlight.

"My father is *dead*," she would say, but it made no difference.

"Hasn't it occurred to you," said her mother, "that they tease you because you rise to it? They're not talking about gypsies, they're just using the word that gets the strongest reaction from you."

Jen said that it hadn't occurred to her.

And then when Melanie took her part and said, "Leave her alone, she can't help being half gypsy," Jen got even angrier. Perhaps because she knew that even if the others weren't talking about gypsies, Melanie was.

She had no idea what had triggered off this particularly strong spate of teasing, but the longer it went on the less able she seemed to be to control her own feelings. It began to colour her whole life, until she could see that she was pouring all her energies into either ignoring them or

2

answering them back, and this increased her anger, because she wanted some of her energies for other things. Then something happened which made everything that had gone before seem like a kind of premonition.

She was on her way home from school. She had stopped near the flyover and leant on the pedestrian barrier to watch the four lanes of traffic. If she half-closed her eyes they seemed to flow by like a river. The noise was the roaring of wind and water and the vehicles up on the flyover were barges on an aqueduct. It was strangely peaceful because the sheer volume of outside noise drove all the noisy thoughts out of her head.

So she was standing there, with her eyes and ears dreamily half-focused, at the very moment that they chose to arrive.

Just as she was enjoying the pleasant sensation of her mind emptying itself of all the half-imagined rubbish—this rubbish became reality. It was almost as if it had all streamed out of her head and taken tangible form in front of her eyes.

And seeing them arrive was the beginning of the real hate.

They came off the motorway in two filthy, clapped-out trucks and two Beetles, each towing a caravan, and parked on the litter-strewn rough grass underneath the flyover. They got out almost at once—four men, three women, and what seemed like hundreds of kids and dogs. They left all the doors of the trucks and cars open and at first didn't do much—just stood around and screamed at the kids and dogs to keep off the road. They never once looked over at her.

While she watched, they unpacked some kind of primus stove. They seemed to be brewing tea. Some of

3

them sat on the ground. An old woman sat down stiffly on the step of her modern caravan. Then one of the men jumped up again and stood as if awaiting something.

Slipping down the motorway exit came an old Ford towing a grubby caravan. It was followed by a dormobile. The man who had jumped up stood with his arms outstretched and guided them on to the wasteland, indicating that they should park beside the next stout leg of the flyover.

The driver of the dormobile got out first. He went straight to the back of the first truck and climbed inside. When he came out he was leading two—no, three—goats. Without taking much notice of anyone else he proceeded to tether them, separately, on the thin littered grass.

They had come to settle.

And she hated them with a hatred so intense that it frightened her.

Part of her wanted to stay and watch them—the other part wanted to leave, not to return until the wasteland had been handed back to the Coke cans and candy wrappers which had squatters' rights there.

She turned away from the barrier and almost bumped into Tom. For a moment she wondered how she could distract his attention from the flyover. But she needn't have bothered because he'd seen already. He nodded across at the site and laughed. "I see your relatives have dropped in," he said.

"Oh yes," said Jen. She pointed over at the goats. "And I see they've brought your relatives with them."

"Cheeky beggar," said Tom amiably, but Jen pushed past him and hurried on home.

She opened the door of the flat, walked into the kitchen and stopped. A girl in a long blue robe with a silver border was standing in front of the small mirror over the sink, holding her dark hair up on top of her head with both hands. At the sound of the door she turned, letting her hair fall down around her shoulders.

"Oh. I didn't recognise you," said Jen.

Her mother laughed, half embarrassed. "I was trying a new style," she said. She gathered her hair in both hands and piled it up again. "What do you think?"

Jen walked forward and tweaked at the blue robe. "Where'd this come from?" she said.

"The boutique. We unpacked six this morning. I couldn't resist it. Do you like it?"

She turned slowly and the graceful folds of the blue robe swayed around her ankles.

"It's a bit film starry," said Jen.

"That's not a compliment, is it?"

Jen sat down at the kitchen table. "Well, I don't know. When do you wear it? It's not quite the thing for washing up in, is it?"

Her mother turned briskly away from her and began to fill the kettle. "I don't spend all my time washing up," she said. "Or even most of it." She lit the gas and banged the kettle down on top of it. "Would you like one?"

"A cup of tea? Yes, please."

"No, Jen! One of these robes. There's another blue one, two purples and a tangerine. Diana's taken the other tangerine." She reached for the caddy and shook some tea into the pot.

"I don't want to wear your clothes," said Jen.

"They're not mine. We bought them in for the boutique."

5

"Well, if they're suitable for you and Diana, they can't be suitable for me, can they?"

"I don't see why not. You're much the same build and colouring as me."

"There is the small matter of the seventeen-year age gap."

"That doesn't mean much with clothes these days. I wouldn't be surprised if we sell the others to girls not much older than you."

"Maybe that means you're a bit old for one then." The kettle was boiling and Jen pushed past her mother, turned off the gas and poured the boiling water into the teapot.

Her mother moved across to the kitchen table and sat at it, with her fingers spread out on the formica top. The sleeves of the robe fell back from her arms. She watched quietly as Jen unhooked the mugs from the edge of the shelf and poured the tea.

"What's gone wrong today?" she said, when her tea was in front of her. "You're very ratty."

Jen sat down across the table from her and stirred her tea into waves whose tips flicked over on to the yellow formica. "As of ten minutes ago," she said, "the waste-land under the flyover is a gypsy encampment."

There was a moment of complete stillness in the room and then her mother let out a long sigh. "Oh," she said.

Jen looked quickly across at her with the slightly distorted face of someone who might begin to cry. "Don't you want to go and join them, then?"

Her mother gazed down into her tea. "It's a little late for that," she said quietly.

"They will be moved on, won't they?" said Jen.

"Oh yes. I expect they'll be moved on."

"Well don't sound like that about it—they can't possibly be allowed to camp there—it's not a suitable place."

"No. It never is."

"Well it's *not*. There's no sanitation—no water—they've made it look like a tip already. And they've got *goats*!"

Quite suddenly her mother began to giggle. "Goats are the last straw, are they?"

"You can't have goats in a *town*."

"Actually you can. They don't need much grazing and they give quite a lot of milk."

"But they smell. And they've got evil eyes. What are you laughing at?"

"I just find it funny that you're so indignant about goats. You sound like a true Gorgio."

"What's that," said Jen automatically, without even bothering to put a questioning inflection into her voice.

"A non-gypsy, as you perfectly well know. Just because you've never seen goats in the town before doesn't automatically mean that they shouldn't be here. They can't smell any worse than the exhaust fumes. And at least it's a live smell."

Jen leant over her tea and tried to trap a minute tea leaf on the end of a fingernail. "Did my—father have goats?"

"No. His people didn't have goats—just the horses. Are there horses under the flyover?"

"No, just filthy old trucks and caravans and goats," said Jen, her anger rising again. "I met Tom and he said 'I see your relatives have come to stay'. Well, they're not *my* relatives."

"It's unlikely."

"They've never come here before, why do they have to come now, of all times?"

"Why is now a specially bad time?"

"Well it *is*. I don't think you understand what it's like. People *know* about me here."

Her mother leant back in her chair and let herself sink a little into the folds of the blue robe. "There's no reason why they shouldn't know," she said. "You haven't got anything to be ashamed of."

Jen scraped back her chair and walked to the window. "*That's* a joke," she said, staring out into the street. Behind her she heard her mother get up and the blue robe swish quickly across the kitchen to the sitting-room door. In the doorway she paused. "You don't have much sense of loyalty, do you?" she said. The sitting-room door slammed behind her.

Jen took out her essay book and sat down at the kitchen table. She opened the book at the first blank page. *The thing that matters most to me*, she wrote, *is hate*. And underlined the last word.

# 2

THE DREAM WAS of such intensity that her own scream woke her up with a feeling as though she had just fallen into her bed from somewhere far above it. For a moment or two she couldn't even sit up but lay as she was, with the hot sweat cooling on her skin, trying to compose her mind in the swirling darkness and to understand again the familiar shapes of her own room. The forms of the furniture, and even of the walls, seemed to flood about in the darkness, pouring into each other and drawing back. It was almost as if she had taken them by surprise and caught them out trying to reshape into their normal, day-time selves.

Quick footsteps approached the door. It opened sharply, banging against the dressing table, and the light was switched on.

Jen and her mother blinked at each other across the brightness. "What was it?" said her mother. "Are you all right?"

Jen half sat up, leaning on one elbow. "Yes, I'm all right," she said unsteadily. She sat up properly and held her hands out in front of her. They were shaking. "Look!" she said.

Her mother stood for a moment. Then crossed over in two steps and sat on the bed. "What's the matter, lovey?" she said. "Was it a dream?"

She looked so normal, bringing light and common sense into the meaningless darkness, that for a moment Jen wanted to reach out and hug her, be comforted like a child. Instead she put her hands up to her head and smoothed her hair back from her face. "Yes, it was just a dream," she said. "Sorry I made a noise."

Her mother half laughed. "I should say you made a noise," she said. "You gave a horrible shriek. My heart's still going like a steam hammer."

"Sorry," said Jen again.

"What were you dreaming about? What could be that bad?"

Jen shook her head. "I can't remember. It's all right. It's gone now. Pity I woke you up."

"Shall I make us a cup of tea?"

"No," said Jen. "Go back to sleep. You'll be tired in the morning."

"You don't want to tell your dream?"

"I can't even remember it."

Her mother got up and moved to the door, her bare feet making a slightly sticky sound on the lino. In the doorway she hesitated. "You don't often have nightmares, do you?"

"I don't usually dream at all," said Jen.

"Everybody dreams. Maybe you just don't remember them?"

"Yes," said Jen. "Goodnight."

Still her mother hesitated. "I could leave the door ajar," she suggested.

"No thanks. I don't want to be blown out of bed by the draught."

Her mother nodded, put out the light and pulled the door to behind her. Jen listened as the footsteps receded to the bed on the far side of the living room; and regretted not having accepted the cup of tea. It might have been nice to have clattered around with kettles and mugs for a while, because, although it was true that she couldn't remember it, the dream was in some way still with her.

She realised that she was afraid of going back to sleep in case the dream was waiting there for her.

She tried to think about it, in order to dispel the fear, but somehow she couldn't. There wasn't anything to think about. There was no story, there were no events. It was a dream that seemed to have risen up from the most ancient part of the brain, where there are no words. And because that primitive part of the brain knows no words, nothing which arises from it can be expressed in words, or thought about with the rational mind.

She switched on the little bedside light and sat up, cross legged, in bed. Such powerful feelings that dream had evoked and yet she had no way to express them, even to herself. She couldn't wrap the fears and feelings in words and send them rolling away. They remained with her.

She put the light out again, pulled the curtains back and pushed up the window. She leant out and breathed in the cold fresh air, looking up and down the street. It was just after three in the morning and there was no one in sight. The full moon struck a dull pewter light from the tarmac of the road. There was no wind and the trees were still.

She looked straight down, three floors, on to the tops of the railings which bordered the building.

And in that moment the building seemed to tip itself

11

forward as if it would throw her out of its window. The sensation was so strong that she gripped the windowsill with both hands. She almost felt as though her body had already fallen out of the window, was flailing through the air, was impaled on that row of black, iron spikes. She thought that she knew exactly how those spikes would feel as they ran into her body—stabbing between the ribs and through the flesh, down her full length.

Sickened at such a morbid thought she drew back from the window, and then, half fascinated, leant slowly forwards and out again, holding tightly to the sill.

The moonlight struck one side of each railing, one side of each point, emphasising its sharpness. And this time it seemed that the two spikes immediately below her were directed precisely towards her eyes. It almost seemed that if she didn't fall on to the railings, they would rush up to meet her and blind her with their sharpness.

Sharpness!

The dream had been of sharpness.

She drew back from the window again, curled down into her bed and buried her face in the softness of the pillow, shutting out the thought, the feel, of those railings.

It had been of single sharpness, the dream, not multiple sharpness, like the railings. It had been to do with something hard and sharp and dangerous which seemed to be seeking her out; hard like metal, cold like ice, pointed like the head of a spear, either very large or very small, either so large that it would impale her and split her in two, or so small as to be invisible and therefore unavoidable. And all around and behind and through the dream was the idea of the gypsies—no pictures, or words, or names, just the flavour of them, like a very faded but recognisable backcloth.

She curled up smaller in the bed and clenched her fists. Her fingernails dug into her palms and at once she straightened out her hands, recoiling from the sharp feeling even though she knew exactly what it was.

When she did sleep, it was uneasily and shallowly. The powerful, wordless dream did not return, but in the morning its flavour was still there.

She was first up. She washed and dressed and then, while her mother was in the bathroom making up her face, she ran down to the main front door and outside. She walked round the building to the side where her bedroom window was, and stood on the pavement, confronting the railings.

They protected such a miserable little strip of land between the base of the building and the pavement that she couldn't see why they had to be there at all. It was such a narrow strip of ground, little more than a foot wide, made up of sour earth, accidental grass and dead ragwort. And there were no gates in the railings at the front of the flats—just a huge opening so that anybody could walk in or out of the block. In fact you could even walk round behind the railings, with no trouble at all, and trespass on the dreary ground they guarded so sternly.

She gripped a railing in each hand and leant back against their strength. They were old and irrelevant and useless, she told them, in her mind, and not worthy of a nightmare. She reached up and stroked the points. They were slightly rounded, they weren't even very sharp. Although, of course, they would be sharp if you fell on them from a height. She drew her hands quickly away and wiped off the cold hard feeling against the sides of her skirt.

She got back to the kitchen before her mother had

finished in the bathroom and put the kettle on for tea. She put her hand into the drawer to find a teaspoon from the jumble of cutlery—and the prong of a fork jabbed her thumb. It didn't even pierce the skin, but for a moment she thought she might faint. A wave of nausea rose from her stomach and everything went black and fuzzy round the edges. She sat down at the table and rubbed her thumb as if she could wipe away the sensation of sharpness.

She had had dreams before—even bad dreams—but dreams that had faded in daylight. Not dreams that spilled over into the real world. She tried to understand it, but couldn't. In one sense there was so little to it—just vicious sharpness against a faint, very faint and distant, vision of the gypsies.

The dream had come with the gypsies. She had never dreamt like this before and they had never been in the town before. And the more she tried to understand it, the more she realised that she believed it was telling her something. Dreams that told you something were prophecies, omens—surely a dream about such a fundamental danger had to be a warning?

The kettle had worked itself to a pitch of hysteria—flinging its lid about, blurting out gouts of boiling water from its spout, half invisible in its cloud of steam.

Jen got up and began to make tea so that she could look normal when her mother came out of the bathroom.

And quite suddenly she felt that she was in danger —perhaps, literally, mortal danger.

# 3

SHE COULD HAVE gone the long way round to school and avoided the flyover altogether. Instead, she went directly to it, crossed the road by the foul-smelling pedestrian underpass and emerged on the periphery of the encampment, by the goats.

The vans and trailers were strung out in a long line away from her, to fit the narrow shape of the available land. Most of the doors were open but the people all seemed to be inside. A group of very small children squatted on the grass between two trucks, playing an elaborate game with pebbles. Two cross-breed dogs, tied near them, pricked their ears at her but didn't bark. In their estimation she had not yet quite set foot on their territory.

The three nanny goats stopped grazing, lifted their heads, and stared unblinkingly at her out of their devil's eyes. They had no horns and in any case their short tethers would not have permitted them to reach her—but they frightened her. Their eyes were round and golden, each pupil a black vertical slit—unreal, like eyes in a mask.

There was no adult in sight and she wouldn't pass the goats.

As she watched, the old woman emerged from the farthest caravan and sat herself carefully on its step, just as she had sat the day before. She was wearing an ordinary, rather long, dress and several cardigans, and had something in her hand which she kept putting to her mouth. She seemed to be looking straight across at Jen, but made no sign that she had seen her. This old woman was from another age, belonging with high-wheeled, painted trailers—horses—woven baskets full of pegs and primroses. The thing she raised so regularly to her mouth was a briar pipe.

The air was cold and unmoving, the sky a matt unbroken grey. The scene was still and empty but Jen, although still, felt full up with tension.

A man walked, quite abruptly, out of the nearest truck. He was about thirty, tall and broad with a red weather-marked face and hair like hay. He saw Jen at once and walked right up to her, between two of the goats, so that she took a step backwards.

He was smiling.

"Hallo, little lady," he said. "Come to visit us?"

Jen opened her mouth, but she had too much to say and it couldn't all come out at once.

"Don't be shy," said the man. "Is it that you're wanting the old mother to tell your fortune?"

A golden labrador puppy appeared from the back of the truck. It paddled across the grass on fat, floppy feet and then sat down sharply. When it sat, sleek golden rolls rested on its haunches. It turned its snubby golden face this way and that, listening and looking.

Poor little thing, Jen thought automatically.

"She will," the man was saying. "You come with me and we'll ask her together."

16

"I don't want to ask her anything," said Jen. "I just want to know how long you're staying."

There was a pause.

The pup rose, turned to sniff its tail and fell over.

"That depends," said the big man. He wasn't smiling any more, but he wasn't frowning yet, either. He didn't understand.

"Because you're not wanted here, you know," said Jen, and her voice came out high and loud, and she clenched her hands, and her nails pressed into her palms and the sharpness was sickening.

The big man turned away from her and began to walk back towards the truck.

"Where are you going?" said Jen, startled at the lack of reaction.

He stopped and half-turned. "About my business," he said. "There's no talking with the likes of you."

Jen was vaguely aware that tears were pouring down her face, yet she was not really crying.

"You're spoiling everything just by being here," she said. "You can't just arrive like this and disrupt everything. If you don't move they'll *make* you move."

"Who's 'they'?"

"The police."

"Go to school," said the gypsy.

Jen had planned what she wanted to say, but it was all gone. Only tears and rage and sharp fingernails were left.

"I don't want you here," she half-screamed at him.

But even then he didn't seem angry. "And have we all got to suffer, then," he said, "because one little girl is unhappy?" And went inside the truck, out of sight, leaving her to the goats.

It was an odd morning at school. She felt partly guilty about the things she had said to the big man, partly angry that he had taken so little notice of her, had called her a 'little girl'. She wasn't really sure what she had expected—she certainly hadn't pictured them hitching up their trailers and driving off at her command. But you had to try—didn't you? You couldn't just grumble, you had to take action as well.

Then she started to get the little sharp pains.

The first one was in her stomach and it struck just as she was told to stand up and read from *Lorna Doone*. In a way it was as well that it did, because her mind had still been under the flyover and she hadn't taken in anything that had happened in the classroom. The pain brought her back to herself, and then standing up and reading took her mind off the pain.

When her turn was over she found that she had earache—or was it an ache in a back tooth? She wasn't sure. Then it wasn't there, anyway, but a sudden sharp little pain stabbed unexpectedly in the middle of her calf. Then she began to feel them everywhere—little twinges in her arms, her legs, her back, her neck—not very severe, but sudden, and surprising.

At the end of the morning she could not even have told which subjects they had been taught. The vicious little stabbing feelings brought back again the horror of the dream and her mind was suddenly full of the idea that somewhere someone was sticking pins into an effigy of her.

The idea commanded all her attention and she wandered home at lunchtime without knowing whether or not she had spoken to anyone at school or been spoken to.

She reached the flyover, half hoping the dirty grass would be empty and half knowing it would not.

The traffic was as dense and noisy as ever, but it didn't entirely block her view of the camp which looked deserted, apart from the goats at the far end and, in the middle, the small golden puppy she had seen that morning.

Even as she looked the pup began to waddle forwards, away from the camp and towards the road. There was no one outside any of the trailers, and no one saw it. No one but Jen, who was the other side of four lanes of traffic. And although she hadn't called to it, or signed to it, and although she was fairly certain it couldn't see her, she felt somehow guilty, as well as appalled, when she realised what it was going to do.

It was going to paddle fatly across the wide busy road towards her.

The passing vehicles were suddenly huge, the drivers, even of the cars, seated too high to notice anything so small. And there was nothing that she could do.

When the pup reached the edge of the far pavement it was no longer clearly in Jen's sights—she could only glimpse it when there was a gap in the traffic that cut through all four lanes. But there were very few gaps.

She glimpsed it again at the pavement edge. It was sitting down. Perhaps it would stay there. Or go back to the caravans. Inside her head she screamed to someone to come out of one of the caravans and notice it.

She glimpsed it again and it was standing up. No one appeared on the site. There was no way that she could have made herself heard above the roaring.

It was off the edge of the kerb and on the road now—and the glimpses came faster and faster so that the pup's progress began to look like a sequence from an old film.

She screwed up her hands into fists and ground them against her jaw. It was too awful to bear. It was so little, so soft, it would be squashed completely flat.

Another glimpse and it had crossed the first lane of traffic. It was sitting down! Sitting, with one lane of traffic racing behind it and three in front. She almost wished someone would kill it quickly and get it over with.

Now it was standing with its back to her, as if it might try to return to the camp.

Jen climbed over the pedestrian barrier and looked in vain for a gap in the traffic that would let her cross to it. The vehicles went by so fast that the wind of their passing blew her hair and coat about. She pressed her back against the barrier. A blue estate car flashed by, and its wing mirror grazed her belt buckle. She and the pup would both be killed.

It was now in the middle of the road and appeared to be heading directly for her.

She waved her arms at the oncoming cars. If one would understand, and stop, and hold up the others until it was safe. . . .

But they were going too fast to see her and she realised that even if one did see her, it would be going too fast to stop safely. It suddenly occurred to her that she was on the verge of causing a tragic accident.

It was very difficult to get back over the barrier. She needed to hitch herself up on to it and swing her legs over, but, working from this side, there was no room to manoeuvre.

She saw a red car coming—he was signalling that he

wanted to change lanes—he was a little farther out from the barrier than the rest—she hitched up, swung over, dropped down just as an articulated lorry thundered by.

The lorry seemed to have dozens upon dozens of wheels, set in pairs, bearing tons of weight—would there be anything at all left of a puppy that met such a creature?

Tired of her old-movie glimpses, she dropped down on all fours on the dirty pavement and peered underneath the traffic. And at that moment two saloon cars passed her, leaving a little more space between them than some, and from out of that space shot the pup, golden and unscathed, and pressed its stubby face to the pedestrian barrier while the great wheels turned behind it.

"Oh, puppy!" said Jen. "Oh, puppy, you have a guardian angel!"

She put her hand to the gap at the bottom of the barrier. "Come on, puppy," she said.

It sniffed her hand, it licked her hand, it wagged its whole body, it flattened itself down and squirmed and splayed its way through to her, under the bottom bar.

When it was through it wriggled, and licked her, and then sat down abruptly. It was tired.

Jen picked it up and stood with it held against the side of her face. "Oh, puppy!" she said. "Your guardian angel must be a nervous wreck. But you're safe now. I'm going to take you home with me, and you don't ever have to go back to those horrible people again."

# 4

"WE CAN'T KEEP him," said her mother, on her hands and knees on the kitchen floor, tickling the fat yellow tummy.

"He's so beautiful," said Jen, sitting back on her heels.

"Yes, but it wouldn't be fair on him—we'd have to leave him alone all day. Anyway, first we must tell the police we've got him. Someone may be looking for him. Then if he's not claimed we'll have to find him a home. Ouch!" The puppy had seized a mouthful of long dark hair and was standing four-square, pulling hard.

"All right," said Jen, helping to wrest the hair out of his mouth. "I'll find him a good home. Probably Tom'll have him."

"He may be claimed."

"No," said Jen. "No one who cared about a dog would let it wander about alone like that."

"I suppose not. But he's well fed. He's fat—and he's not hungry. That was good stewing steak he turned his nose up at."

The puppy sat and looked complacently about him.

"I must get back," said Jen. "Can I leave him here this afternoon—until I find somewhere?"

"All right. But you can clean up the widdle. Jen, you've hardly eaten anything."

"I'm not hungry."

"You . . ."

". . . must eat. I know. I'll eat tonight."

She gathered up some old newspapers from the shelf under the sink and went through into her room.

"Come on, puppy," she called, spreading the papers on the floor.

He came, wagging, for a game, but set up a pitiful wail when he realised he was to be shut in alone.

"You see," said her mother. "We couldn't do that to him every day. Come on—we've both got to go. At least he's safe from the traffic in there."

From behind the door the puppy's next wail accused them both of heartless betrayal.

They clutched at each other like two small children in distress.

"Oh, look, I *can't* take him to the boutique," said Jen's mother.

"It's all right," said Jen. "It's only a couple of hours till I get back. Block your ears and run!"

They chased each other out of the flat with their hands over their ears and ran down the stairs giggling a little. A desolate wail pursued them as far as the first landing. Guiltily, they put their hands over their mouths instead of over their ears.

They parted at the front door making anxious faces at each other.

"I'll find him a good home," Jen reassured her mother's retreating back. Without looking round, her mother raised a hand in acknowledgement and hurried on, half running, to relieve a hungry Diana at the boutique.

Jen cornered Tom when school came out.

"Hey, do you want a dog?" she said.

"I've got a dog."

"I know. I mean another dog. Only I've found one—it's a stray and we can't keep it because we're both out all day. Oh Tom, it's only a puppy and it's so beautiful."

"What sort?"

"I'm not sure. It might be a labrador."

"My Mum might not like another dog."

"Two wouldn't be much more bother than one."

Tom laughed. "Oh sure. You've never kept a dog, have you?"

"We can't keep it—and it has to go somewhere. It deserves a happy life."

"We all deserve that—doesn't mean we get it."

"Can I just bring it round and show you?"

He considered. "All right, if it really needs a home, I'll take it. Then if Mum can't cope, or Fred eats it or something, I might be able to get my uncle to have it."

Jen beamed. If the pup at least could be rescued and given a happy future, everything else seemed more bearable. "I'll go and get it and bring it to your house," she said.

"I'll come back with you now and collect it."

"No. I'll bring it."

"That's stupid. Why don't we go and get it at once?"

"No. My mother'll be expecting me to come in and have something to eat, like usual."

"I have seen people eating before. I won't go berserk or anything."

"She won't have enough to offer you any."

"I don't want any. I got my own to go home to."

"She'll be embarrassed if you come round unexpectedly and she hasn't enough food."

"I don't think your mother embarrasses that easily."

Jen had a sudden, vivid, mental picture of the girl in the blue flowing robe. "Why do you keep wanting to come and see my mother?"

"I *don't*. I'm offering to pick up this dog you want me to have."

"I'll bring it," said Jen, "later on." And walked briskly away.

The puppy greeted her with hysterical joy. She cleared away the wet newspapers, peeled some potatoes and had settled down to play with him, ignoring all homework including the essay, when she heard her mother's footsteps on the stairs. She didn't come straight in because she was stopped on the landing by Mrs Herratt, who bounced out of her next door flat like a ping-pong ball.

Jen could hear their voices clearly.

"I wanted to catch you, dear, and warn you," said Mrs Herratt. "Have you seen what's coming along the road?"

"No?"

"I don't suppose I have to tell you," said Mrs Herratt, "that we've now got gypsies in the town for our sins. One of them's out there. I've been watching her. She's been in to each block and she stays inside for well over half an hour. She must be knocking on the doors of all the flats. She's right in the next block at the moment, so I've just come to say to you, dear, keep your door shut."

25

"If someone knocks, I usually open up to see what they have to say," said Jen's mother calmly.

"Well, you let in a gypsy, dear, and you'll let in a lot of trouble."

Jen got up quickly. She had been sitting on her heels and one of her feet had gone to sleep. She limped uncomfortably across to the kitchen window and the voices on the landing faded for her. She looked out and down.

A figure was just emerging from the next door block, foreshortened from this angle, made fat by numerous cardigans, but unmistakeable. The old gypsy woman had left the step of her modern caravan and was slowly, steadily, scouring the neighbourhood. For what? Was she looking for people whose fortunes she could tell and so make a little money? Or was she looking for someone who had carried off a small yellow dog?

An extraordinary mixture of guilt and fear clotted itself together in Jen's chest.

The impassive figure of the old gypsy made its way towards the main door of the flats and disappeared inside. At the same time, Jen's mother walked into the kitchen and shut the door firmly behind her.

Jen thought, "How much time have I got? If the downstairs flats are empty, which they probably are at this time of day, she could be up here in minutes."

She watched as her mother dumped her armful of paper bags on to the kitchen table and bent to stroke the head of the pup. Then she scooped him up and carried him towards her room. "I've done the potatoes," she said over her shoulder. "I'll put him in my room till we've eaten so that he doesn't get under your feet. I'm taking him to Tom's later. He'll have a nice home there."

"All right," said her mother. She didn't make any

further enquiries. She looked tired. "Do you want a cup of tea before I start the food?" she said.

"No thanks."

Jen went into her room and shut the door. The puppy had cried most of the afternoon, greeted Jen ecstatically, played wildly, and he was exhausted. He allowed himself to be lifted on to the bed where he flopped down and slept.

Moments later, Jen heard the quiet knock on the front door to the flat.

She sat on her bed beside the sleeping dog and the sounds which came through her closed bedroom door told her what was happening. Her mother had refused the offer of having her palm read but had brought the old woman in for a cup of tea. She couldn't hear the words but she could hear the quiet hum of conversation.

The puppy heard it, too. He twitched his ears in his sleep, then woke and sat up. He listened, at first drowsily, then intently with his ears piled on top of his head in an almost exaggerated expression of interest. He made his way unsteadily to the edge of the bed, flopped down on to the floor and went to the door. He began to blow and sneeze under it, to whine, to scrabble with his fat paws.

Jen picked him up and tried to comfort him, to distract him, but he struggled in her arms and yelped with frustration.

In the other room her mother raised her voice and called, "Let him out. He won't bother us."

Jen put the puppy down on the floor. Her eyes filled with tears so that the little yellow form was just a blur.

"Oh you fool puppy," she whispered to him. "You fool, fool, fool puppy."

She opened the door.

Her mother was sitting in a chair facing her across the room. The old woman was sitting with her back to Jen's door, but all twisted round in her chair, looking over her shoulder with interest.

The puppy scuttered across the lino to her. She put her teacup on the floor and bent stiffly forward to greet him. "Ah, my little one," she said. "Where have you been?"

Jen's mother glanced quickly from her daughter to the old woman who had lifted the puppy on to her knee. He stood on his hindlegs to lick her face and she beamed at him and rubbed his back with curled, arthritic fingers.

"Is he yours?"

"Oh yes. I was going to ask if you'd seen him. I've been asking everyone. We missed him dinner time. We couldn't find him nowhere, we made sure he'd been killed on that road. The little girl's been crying her heart out."

"This is my daughter," said Jen's mother. "She found him—she thought he was a stray."

"Bless your pretty face. You're a good girl," said the old woman, and looked directly at Jen with little black eyes which glittered but did not seem to recognise.

Jen stood rigidly in her doorway and said nothing.

"I must go," said the gypsy, struggling to her feet, clutching the dog which was stretching upwards to chew her ear. "I must take him back. He's me little grand-daughter's, you see, and she's so unhappy. Now you're sure you don't want your future told? I could come back."

"No, thank you," said Jen's mother.

"You've a lucky face," said the gypsy, falling back into the role she felt was expected of her. "Good things will happen. I think I'll see you again."

Jen's mother closed the door behind the old figure and turned round. A very faint aroma of tobacco hung on the air.

"Did you know it was their dog?" she said.

Jen started to turn away from her, but there was a fresh tap at the door. Her mother's hand was still on the latch. She pulled it open.

"My, that was quick," said Mrs Herratt. "Are you all right, dear?"

"Yes. Why wouldn't we be?"

"I heard you let that gypsy in. I've been worrying about you."

Jen's mother turned away from the door and went to pick up the teacups. "An old woman with sore feet came in for a rest," she said. "I don't think we were in much danger."

"I peeped out as she was going," said Mrs Herratt. "She had a little dog with her. I swear she didn't have that when she was coming down the road."

"Jen found it straying. It was a lucky chance that the old woman came to the flat and recognised it."

"You shouldn't have let her take it," said Mrs Herratt.

"It was hers."

Jen's mother carried the cups out to the kitchen, but Mrs Herratt followed her through, leaving the front door open.

"Nonsense. That's an old one. Anybody could say that and the dog couldn't tell you no different, could it? She'll sell it."

Slowly, Jen followed them through. Her mother was rinsing the cups under the tap.

"It's not actually hers," she was saying, "it belongs to her grand-daughter. She's only a little girl and she

29

and her dog have been crying for each other all afternoon."

"Oh well, if you like to believe that," said Mrs Herratt.

Leaning in the doorway, resting her head against the unpleasantly sharp edge of the jamb, Jen said, "It is their dog. I saw it at the camp."

Her mother, drying the cups, didn't look across at her. "So you see, Mrs Herratt," she said, "in fact we stole the dog from them."

"I *didn't* steal it! It wandered away from the camp itself. I only picked it up to save it from being run over."

"But you didn't take it back to them, did you?" said her mother, smiling in a particular way, speaking with an exaggerated lightness. Jen knew that anger was very close. "You and Mrs Herratt seem to have decided that they have no right to their own dog."

"They'll eat it," said Mrs Herratt darkly. "You'll find they'll put it in a pot and boil it up."

"I'm sure you're right," said Jen's mother. "That's why they don't often have horses nowadays—they ate the lot. They're quite insatiable, you know."

Mrs Herratt looked thoughtfully at her for a moment. "I know what I've heard," she said.

"Of course," said Jen's mother. "I mean they can't expect to keep these things secret, can they? I wouldn't go too near the encampment if I were you. After they've finished the dogs and the goats and their own children, they'll probably start on the passers-by."

Mrs Herratt gazed down at her feet, trying to decide whether to take offence or not. "Oh well, dear," she said at last, "you're bound to be upset by their presence. We all know about your past, but it's over and forgotten,

30

now. You don't have to defend them." And, wisely, she left the flat.

Jen's mother looked quickly across at her and away. "Have you noticed," she said, "what nice company you and your opinions keep?"

# 5

"I think i'm going to die," she said to Tom.

"There's a lot of it about," said Tom impassively. He had turned his chair round so that he sat with his back to the deskful of homework. Jen sat on the edge of the bed with Fred draped across her feet and snoring softly. "And don't shuffle. You'll disturb my dog."

"That's not a dog," said Jen, looking quite fondly down at Fred. "It's a rug. And an old rug at that."

"The rug of ages," said Tom.

"You can laugh," said Jen. "I don't think you'd care if I died."

"I expect I would. It would depend."

"What on?"

"I don't know. I'd care if you'd just eaten a pork chop because then I could have had it instead."

"All men are heartless."

"I'm not a man."

"I suppose you will be, one day."

"Haven't decided. I might rather be an orang-utan."

"You've got the face for it."

"Thank you. And what are you going to be? A fortune teller?"

Jen stood up sharply and Fred snorted to his feet and shook himself. She didn't go out of the room but stood glowering at the large poster of Tecumseh on the inside of Tom's door. "I wish you'd all shut up about it," she said. "I don't know what you're on about."

"Catch!" said Tom and, automatically, she turned and put out her hand. Something glittered through the air and landed with a smack on her palm. It was a five penny piece. "I've crossed your palm with silver," he said in a wheedling voice. "Won't you tell me my future?"

Jen looked at him. There was no malice in his face but, almost as a reflex action, she threw the coin straight at it, as hard as she could. Tom ducked, and it hit the wall behind his head and clattered down on to the back of the desk. Tom straightened up, laughing. "What kind of a future is that?" he said.

"You wouldn't have a future at all if I had my way," said Jen, leaning back against Tecumseh. "I'd like to see you take a very long walk on a very short pier."

"Oh well," said Tom, sighing heavily. "If you won't tell a fortune for a friend—I'll just have to go and visit our new neighbours and ask your Gran instead."

"She is *not* my Gran," Jen almost screamed at him. "I haven't got a Gran. She's got nothing to do with me. She's a horrible, smelly old woman and she's taken that poor little dog away with her. Why won't you believe me that I hate them? I went down there before school today and told them to clear off."

"Didn't have much effect, did you?" He sprawled in his chair. Fred had laid his shaggy head on one knee, demanding comfort for his rude awakening, and Tom scratched him behind one ear without looking away from Jen.

"Well, they wouldn't be likely to go just because I told them to, would they? But I had to try something and it wasn't particularly easy. They're frightening. The man was frightening—that old hag's frightening—the goats are frightening. *Now* why are you laughing—why do goats make everyone laugh?"

"I don't know why you get so upset. I don't care if your Dad's a gypsy."

"My dad isn't anything. He's dead! He's always been dead. They killed him if you want to know. They stabbed him to death with a great long sharp knife—and I hadn't even been born then—I've never been in the world at the same time as him—he has nothing to do with me—"

"O.K.," said Tom. "O.K. O.K. O.K. Forget I spoke. You don't have to get hysterical. Think about something else."

"How *can* I?"

"There are more important things in the world than whether or not you get teased about your Dad."

"What's more important than them trying to kill me? I think they've done something."

"Like what? Poisoned your water supply?"

"No. Something peculiar. I think that's why they came. Why else *should* they suddenly come just there—they never have before."

"They know you, then? They really are relatives, are they?"

"No! I've told you, no!"

"Well why would they come here to put a curse on you if they don't even know you? You're paranoid. Why don't you feel sorry for someone other than you for a change? Look at him, there. Try feeling sorry for him—it shouldn't be hard."

"Who's he?"

"Tecumseh. A Shawnee chief."

"What's his problem, then?" said Jen, more aggressively than she meant to.

"His problem was that he lived at the beginning of the nineteenth century and he had to watch the systematic destruction of the entire Indian culture by the whites."

"Oh," said Jen. "Yes." She moved away from the door and the sternly reproachful stare of the dead chief. She felt tired and a little sick. "But I don't see how that helps me."

"I'm giving you something else to think about," said Tom. "I thought it might do you good to think about people worse off than you are. How would you cope if you had to watch your whole way of life destroyed —your freedom of movement restricted—the land, which you *knew* belonged to everybody, fenced off by the whites. . . ."

He reached down with one hand and pulled out the bottom drawer of his desk while still sitting with his back to it. His face had changed. He looked odd and preoccupied. The drawer was mostly full of notebooks, but there were published books in there, too.

"Why do you keep books in a drawer?" said Jen. "Why not on a shelf?"

"These are special," said Tom simply. He pulled one out and opened it at a page marked with a strip of paper. Other strips of paper hung out from between other pages. "Listen," he said. And read, 'Where today is the Pequot? Where are the Narragansett, the Mohawks, the Pohanshet, and many other once powerful tribes of our people? They have vanished before the avarice and the oppression of the white man, as snow before a summer sun.' Doesn't that make you feel something? Something other than self-pity, I mean."

"That's all over now," said Jen. "It's past."

"It isn't. How can it be while there are still Indians alive today? Listen," and he read from another page, 'Every year our white intruders become more greedy, exacting oppressive and overbearing. . . . Wants and oppression are our lot.'" He squinted up at Jen. "'Are we not being stripped day by day of the little that remains of our ancient liberty?'"

Jen turned her back on him and traced the lines of Tecumseh's forehead with her finger. "I don't understand you," she said. "I'm not sure that you're talking about Indians."

"This is an Indian talking," said Tom. "That Indian, in fact. Want to hear another?" His fingers searched through the book, moving from one marker paper to another. Then he read, "'If the Great Spirit wanted men to stay in one place he would make the world stand still; but he has made it to always change, so birds and animals can move and always have green grass and ripe berries. . . .'"

"Oh shut up," said Jen. "If that's how you think why do you go on at me about my father?"

"Because you look funny when you get cross."

"*That's* a pathetic . . ."

"Anyway," said Tom. "They can't move the gypsies on, so they'll probably be there for the rest of your life. Did you know that?"

"Why can't they?"

"Well—have you ever wondered why there's so much land under the flyover? It's the town's common land, would you believe. It was declared common land by

36

some old guy at the end of the nineteenth century who used to own it. One Benjamin Spencer. He can't have been very rich because it's not much land really. Anyhow—the gypsies can't be moved on under the Highways Act because it's common land—And what's really funny is that no one wants to look into the bequest too carefully in case they find the flyover shouldn't be there at all."

"Is this all true?" said Jen.

"Yup."

"How do you know?"

"My mum and dad are members of the Residents' Association, and when they and the other local fascists tried to get the gypsies moved on they were told it was all a very 'delicate situation'. Don't you find it funny? Don't you have any sense of humour?"

The front door slammed and footsteps travelled into the living room and, almost immediately, out again.

"Tom!" said a voice from the foot of the stairs.

"Here."

"Dad says you've got Jen up there."

"She's here."

"Well, she can just come right down again."

Jen flung open the door and stamped down the stairs. Tom followed her with Fred flopping down by his feet, as relaxed as an empty nightdress case.

"Now you know I won't have the two of you up there in that room by yourselves. If you want to talk to each other you can just come and sit in the front room, like anybody else."

"How are you, Mrs Welsh?" said Jen flatly.

"As well as can be expected."

Mrs Welsh's legs had to support quite a lot of weight

37

and had broken out in varicose veins as a protest. For fear of being told about the progress of these, Jen said hurriedly, "And Mr Welsh?"

"He's not getting any younger. And how's this beautiful mother of yours I keep hearing about?"

"Why do you hear about her?" said Jen, startled out of her irritation.

"Tom passes the boutique on his way home from school," said Mrs Welsh a little acidly. "I always have to hear what your mother's wearing. Ah well—I expect you and I could look beautiful if we had those lovely clothes to choose from, couldn't we?"

"Goodbye," said Jen.

"I'm not sending you home," said Mrs Welsh. "I'm simply saying I want you both down here and not shut away upstairs."

"I was going home anyway," said Jen. She wanted to sound dignified but she heard her own voice and it sounded more peevish than anything else. "There's no peace anywhere."

And didn't quite dare to slam the front door.

# 6

IT WAS SOME form of armour-plating. There was nothing else in the picture to give an idea of size. Yet the armour obviously covered a large area—larger than the body of a man. The plates overlapped, for freedom of movement. There was no movement at the moment, yet there was potential movement. The armour was convex in form; seemed to be organic; filled up the whole dream, leaving no space for anything else, not even a meaning.

Jen woke herself up as dramatically as she had woken from the dream of sharpness. And her mother arrived in the room as promptly as she had before.

"They're sending dreams," said Jen, sitting up in bed, very white and hollow-eyed. "They've put a curse on me!"

Her mother moved across and sat on the edge of the bed, just as she had before. "Wake up," she said gently. "You're still dreaming."

"I'm not—you don't know—oh—this is horrible—"

Her mother stood up. "Come on," she said briskly. "Come in to the kitchen and have some tea. If we've got to be up in the night, we might as well enjoy it."

She turned and padded away into the living room,

which at night looked like the bedsitter it was, with the fitted cover off the divan and the bedclothes tumbled about.

Numbly, Jen zipped herself into her woolly dressing gown and padded through after her. She felt even worse than she had after the first dream. She felt as though someone had put all her emotions into a tin can full of nails and had shaken them thoroughly, in fact was still shaking them.

Her mother lit the oven and left the door open. Then put the kettle on. She was wearing the blue robe over her nightdress. "Poor old Jen," she said conversationally. "I hope these nightmares aren't going to happen too often. Bad for both our nerves."

"They'll go on as long as the gypsies are there. They've got to be made to go."

Her mother was setting out mugs, rattling in the cutlery drawer, reaching down the tea caddy. "The travellers have nothing to do with your dreams," she said.

"They have! And I know how to drive them out. I'm going to go to all the houses in the area and tell the people to refuse to give them water."

She hadn't planned to do, or even to threaten, that. The sentence seemed to come out by itself.

Her mother turned round quite slowly and stared at her. Most of the colour seemed to have gone from her face. "That is an appalling—vicious—idea," she said. Her voice was entirely cold. Jen had never seen her look so deeply shocked.

Partly to justify herself, but chiefly because she believed it, she said, "They've put a curse on me—the dreams are—they're sending them. They're a part of it."

"Do you mean one of them actually said something?"

40

"That old woman. When you had her in here."

"What did she say?"

"She said I had a pretty face."

"How can that be a curse?"

"Because I haven't! Don't you ever look at me? I'm ugly. No wonder Tom prefers you. I'm dark and swarthy and ugly, like them."

"Don't *you* ever look at *me*? I've got dark hair. I've got dark eyes. I've got olive skin. Your father had hair like straw. You get your colouring from me."

"Yes, I look at you. And I don't like it. You shouldn't dress up all the time and make your face up all the time. You're supposed to be my mother. Tom fancies you and I think that's revolting."

"So I'm not a mother because I'm not fat and old? What do you think mothers are? They're only women who've had children. And if they love their children and do their best for them, then they're good mothers, thank you."

"But you don't care that they want to kill me!"

"You're just being stupid and I've no patience with it." She turned her back and crouched in front of the fridge making her choice from among three half empty bottles of milk.

"If you think it's stupid to be frightened of dying . . ."

"We've all got to die sometime."

Jen sat down crookedly on the kitchen chair. "I know that! That's why I feel trapped. And by the time I die you won't even be there to help me."

"I thought the travellers were supposed to be killing you by remote control any minute now. In which case I certainly plan to outlive you." She stood up, turned from the fridge and looked across at Jen. Then she put down

41

the milk bottle, stepped quickly across and squatted down by Jen's chair. "I'm sorry, lovey," she said. "Are you really frightened?"

"Mm," said Jen, pressing her lips tightly together. She wondered why people were told to keep a stiff upper lip. The upper lip was never a problem, it was the lower one that got out of control so easily.

Her mother reached out and took both Jen's hands between hers. "Look, exactly what is it that you're frightened of?" she said. "Is it really that you're frightened of the travellers, or is it that you've just started to think about death?"

"Don't know," said Jen. Her voice sounded peculiar, and the second word came out easily an octave higher than the first. She took her hands back and used the palms to scrape the hair off her forehead. She always expected to find it easier to think once the odd wisps had been cleared away. In practice, though, it didn't actually make much difference.

"I don't think death can be so awful," said her mother. "It's so very normal. Everyone's either done it or is going to do it. Every thing and every one who is alive now is going to die sometime."

"That's *horrible*," said Jen. "That's like saying we're all standing beside our own open graves."

"I don't think that would be a very practical way to spend your life."

"That *is* how we spend our lives. We're trapped by it. I don't see that there's any point in doing anything once you see that you're going to die anyway. I mean, eating's only putting off death, isn't it?"

"I see. So as you know you're going to go to bed at night, what's the point of getting up in the morning?"

42

"Yes. What *is* the point?"

"The point is that there's a time for everything."

"You're going to quote the Bible at me now!"

"You quote it! You were the one who learnt that bit last term. I remember you parading around the flat reciting the whole thing. Didn't you listen to what you were saying? Go on, say it now."

Jen did the hair-scraping gesture again and said, half sulkily, "'To every thing there is a season, and a time to every purpose under the heaven.'"

"Go on."

"'A time to be born and a time to die; a time to plant, and a time to pluck up that which is planted.' It doesn't help."

"It should. You're looking at death from the wrong place in your time. You're young and fit—of course you see death as something to be avoided if at all possible. That attitude is part of your health. It's what makes you take reasonable care of yourself—not walk over cliffs or under cars. And when it is time for you to die, I truly believe that death will seem a very different thing to you, in its own season. A very normal thing."

"You're saying I shouldn't think about it now at all?"

"I'm not saying that. Of course you should think about things. But just understand, when you think about that, that you're thinking about it from the wrong place and that this will colour your views. Anything grossly out of place can seem horrifying. There's nothing nasty about people's arms and legs, but I wouldn't want to see an arm lying about all by itself, thank you very much. I know I'm over-simplifying, but I do believe what I'm telling you. There's nothing wrong with the reality of death —but there is something very wrong with spending your

43

whole life fearing it. Because that's not reality, that's imagination—which is almost always far more frightening than reality."

"But I *know* that it will come."

"You know that Thursday will come, that doesn't mean you shouldn't get the best you can out of Wednesday. I can tell you now that I'm going to cook spaghetti for tomorrow night. That doesn't mean you have to spend the whole of the day sitting with your hands folded in your lap and waiting for your helping. Hm? Let the travellers be, Jen. They've got nothing to do with this. It's just that their presence has made you think about your father more, and thinking about him you've begun to think about death for the first time. That's all that's happening."

"That might not be all that's happening. Gypsies were at the start of my life, perhaps they have to be in on the end of it, too. Perhaps I've got to die soon because I shouldn't be here at all."

"Why shouldn't you?"

"I've spoilt your life by being here. You think it's my fault you never married anyone else."

"I do *not*." She released Jen's hands and stood upright, staring down at her as if she didn't quite recognise her.

"You told Diana so."

"I never did. Jen, you're a liar."

"Don't call me that."

"Don't give me cause."

"You did tell Diana. I heard you. I remember exactly what you said. You said, 'There's nothing like having a small child around to put a man off'."

"I don't remember saying that. It must have been years ago."

"It was."

"And you've harboured it all this time?"

"Yes, because you made me feel guilty for existing."

"How you can *say* that! When the only thing that kept me going was having you to care about. When he died the one consolation I clung to was that at least I was pregnant. Even though there are times when I could hit you, I love you and I need you—and whether you like it or not, you're half him. Even though you hardly know what he was like."

"You've told me what he was like."

"I used to, when you were little. But from the time you were about seven you wouldn't listen. You can't even have listened before, or you'd know more."

"Just at the moment I know enough. I still know they want to kill me. They killed him, didn't they?"

"He was killed in a fight with his cousin. 'They' didn't kill him. And anyway, he *was* 'them'."

"Why did his cousin want to kill him?"

"I don't think he did. They had a fight—his cousin had a knife. I think he only meant to hurt him."

"Why did they have to fight at all?"

The kettle had been boiling, ignored, for some time. A long, flat cloud of steam was beginning to form against the wall above the cooker. Her mother turned to spoon tea into the pot, working with her back towards Jen. "They were fighting about me," she said.

"Oh, how romantic," said Jen viciously. "Why did you pick the dead one?"

Her mother slammed the tea caddy down so hard that the spoon leapt out on to the floor, and spun round. "If I didn't think you'd been really frightened, I'd slap your face," she said.

"All right, all right. Don't talk to me any more. I'm not interested." She got up and crossed to switch off the gas under the kettle. She had quite shocked herself and it was in her mind that the best thing to do was to go back to bed.

As she put the kettle out of its misery, her mother's hand shot out and grasped her by the wrist. "Sit down again!" She pushed Jen towards the kitchen chair with such force that Jen staggered. "Go on sit! I don't care if you're interested or not, you're going to listen. I loved your father. Can you understand that—or are you feeling so mean and small at the moment that that seems funny to you? I loved him more than you think you love Tom. Shut up and listen.

"We wanted to get married, but his people were against it and my people were against it. My parents didn't think he was good enough for me. And his didn't think I was good enough for him. Are you taking this in? They thought I wasn't good enough because I was a Gorgio—and because I was expecting you. They're puritanical people. They expect brides to be virgins.

"We were both prepared to break away from our families—although the break would have been far harder for him because he was going to live my kind of life, settled, in a flat, this flat. He was going to give up everything—for me, and for you. But his cousin began insulting me—calling me names. And he couldn't take that so he fought and he was stabbed. I went with him in the ambulance. He was crying—not because of pain but because of what would become of me and our child. He died before we got to the hospital.

"He was eighteen years old, Jen.

"I know things haven't been as comfortable as they

might. It's never comfortable to be brought up without a father. It's never comfortable to be teased about your background. That's why I've let things go—I could see you found it easier at school to say 'I hate gypsies, too' and I thought it didn't matter. But I was wrong, it does matter. And I'm not going to take any more of it from you. You're old enough to understand, and you're old enough to stand up for yourself and not always take the easy way out. I'm sick of your self-pity and I'm sick of wondering what he would think if he could hear his daughter now. Intolerant—prejudiced—narrow-minded—"

She leant back against the cooker and looked at Jen. A lot of the anger had been burnt up. She looked more hurt than anything else.

Jen sat on her hard wooden chair with her arms folded across her stomach, and rocked herself slightly, to and fro.

There was a silence.

Then she raised her head and looked across at her mother through a blur of tears. Even through the blur she could see that her mother's eyes were bright with moisture.

Jen wanted to cross the kitchen and put her arms round the girl who stood on the other side of it. But she wasn't sure what the reaction would be and anyway she felt embarrassed.

At last, "It's not my fault that I never knew him," she said, which wasn't what she wanted to say at all, and had nothing to do with what she was feeling. It was just that it was the only series of sounds she could think of to make in order to break a silence which had become too intense to bear.

It did break it, though not in the best way. Her mother relaxed her shoulders downwards in a sigh. She looked tired and disappointed. "We'd better go to bed," she said. "We can't go on like this."

Jen wanted to keep talking, to precipitate a reunion, but she didn't know what to say. She followed through into the sitting room. "I won't sleep," she tried.

"Yes, you will," said her mother.

Jen continued through into her own room and shut the door slowly, slowly got into bed. And was so worn out that she hardly had time to cry before she slept.

# 7

THE SHARPNESS REARED up and then somehow receded. The armour-plating appeared solid, yet was able to flow about until it took up a shape, a particular form, definite yet indistinct, like something seen at dusk. She couldn't make out what it was, or where it was in relation to her, and somehow she didn't believe that it knew, either.

Even as she dreamt, she realised that the two earlier dreams had been of two aspects of this same thing; and that now she was dreaming it in its entirety. She woke up with the realisation still very clear in her mind.

She sat up in bed. The dawn light was just beginning to show through the thin curtains. She pulled them aside and knelt on the bed to look out. Just for one irrational moment she half thought that she would see the creature she had dreamt moving about on the ground below her window. But the street was empty.

She left the curtains back and held her hands out experimentally in front of her. They were shaking slightly. But although the dream had been frightening, it had not brought that peculiar feeling of primitive terror that she had felt before. She thought about it, trying to work out why, and decided it was because this time, in dreaming the whole creature, she had been using the rational part of her mind. The dream had floated upwards to a level where she could think about it in words.

Having gone so far, she felt quite logical and calm, but then when she tried to go further, fear set in again. Why would they make her dream a big animal—a big animal that had some kind of dangerously sharp horn or claw? Because despite everything her mother had said she knew, as surely as she knew anything, that the dreams were connected with the gypsies. They were building up some animal in her head, and now it was complete, and going to sleep at night suddenly seemed a dangerous thing.

She had got the impression, even while she was still dreaming, that it was somehow casting around, searching—but for what? For her? And if so, what would happen when it found her?

Then—No, she decided, that was not the right way to think. A dream couldn't harm you unless you let it. It was silly to be frightened because that was obviously what they wanted.

The dream was already slightly less frightening now that she knew she was dreaming a creature rather than nameless, wordless, sharpness and bulk. So the thing to do, obviously, was to try to understand it even more fully—to find out exactly what kind of creature it was. She wished she could picture it more clearly. Perhaps if she drew it. . . .

After all, it was possible that they hadn't sent it purely to frighten her—it was possible that it was indeed a warning, as she had thought at first, and if that was so then it was vital to know what the creature was in order to understand the warning.

It's an allegory, she thought. And I hate allegories. But I'll solve it and then I'll know what it is they're warning me about, or threatening me with, and I'll go to them and tell them that I understand. And then we can deal with the whole thing openly and not inside my head.

The compulsion to draw the creature was now quite strong.

She got out of bed and went to her satchel. She found a pencil but no spare paper. So she tore the unfinished essay out of its exercise book and turned it over so that she could draw on the back. Her feet were getting cold, so she hopped back into bed and propped the ruled paper against her small atlas. She gazed at the lined paper in the pale grey morning light.

It was a peculiar shape, this thing, she thought. Obviously a mythical creature. She would take her drawing with her to the library tomorrow and she would look it up in a book and find out just what it was.

But the drawing, when she had done it, was disappointing. The vision she had seen in her dream was so hazy and dim that it was very difficult to think where to put a line on the paper. So in the end she just shaded in what she felt to be the solid areas and ended up with what looked almost like a cloud formation. It had this sharp spike, but it wasn't a unicorn—it didn't have horse's legs and anyway, now that she was remembering more clearly, she realised the spike was at the back. The general outline was long and low and yet it wasn't a dragon. It certainly wasn't a griffon. Perhaps it was a chimera—she couldn't begin to remember what a chimera looked like. Or a yale. A yale was one of the queen's beasts but she couldn't remember ever having seen a picture of one. And yet, after all, perhaps it was a dragon of sorts. It had the right long, serpentine shape, and some dragons do have viciously sharp tails, with arrow heads on them, like the devil's tail.

She had rather hoped she would be able to show the drawing to the librarian and ask what it was—perhaps saying it was a copy of something she had noticed carved somewhere. But she could see now that the drawing wouldn't look like anything at all to a person who had not seen the original image.

I'll look it up under dragons, she decided, because that's what it must be. And felt vaguely dissatisfied with the decision.

Then she noticed that the creature had no eye. In her imagination there was no eye, either, but on paper it looked odd and blind and somehow 'blunt' without one. So she put one in. Just a dot, a single dot.

And for one moment, which soon passed, had a very odd feeling—as if she had done something of immense significance.

As if there was enormous power in that one, minute dot.

# 8

THE NEXT DAY Jen was so preoccupied, at home and at school, that she wasn't really aware if she was teased or not. Except, of course, for the time when she was asked to hand in her essay and she said she had lost it. She was given detention, whether for being careless or for lying, she wasn't sure. Usually the rest of the class were sympathetic if you got detention—but a hoarse voice from the back of the room said, "I bet it was about them Gyppos." And she heard Melanie's high, indignant voice from beside her shouting back, "It was not! She wouldn't write about people like that." Jen kept her head down and refused to acknowledge what was happening. So she never knew if Tom joined in or not.

She was the only one in detention, where she was given half an hour to write the essay again. This time she wrote a prim, stilted, boring piece about being grateful she had enough to eat and a roof over her head, which the English teacher accepted without comment.

By the time she set out for the Library it was nearly dark, and by the time she got there, it was. She hurried gratefully into the warm building from the cold autumn air and pushed her way through the swing doors into the Reference Library.

The librarian was kind but abstracted, and not interested in dragons. "You want the Children's Library," he said, "through there."

"I don't want a story book," said Jen patiently. "I want to look something up—it's a design I've come across. I want to check what kind of a dragon it is."

"Well we've got nothing about dragons in here," he said. "There's no standard reference work so far as I know." He wasn't being patronising, just stating the position as he saw it. "You might well find something in the Children's Library—or if you go through to the Lending Library you might find something among the Art books. Sorry I can't be more help."

"All right," said Jen. "Thank you."

The Children's Library was in a room which opened straight off the Lending Library. It was bright and clean and the floor smelt of wax. The librarian was at the far end, seated not at her desk but at an absurdly small table with, Jen noticed suddenly, three of the gypsy children, a little boy and two girls who looked like his older sisters.

Jen turned her back on them and began to search the shelves of fantasy.

The librarian was trying to teach the children to read. Heels drumming on the crossbar of his chair, the small boy kept up a steady prattle. The two girls were half attending to their lesson, but really they wanted to play, or be left in peace to look at the pictures. Jen remembered the feeling of those laborious beginnings, before you realised what reading could mean.

The books on dragons were, as she had thought they would be, story books for quite young children. The illustrations were modern and showed dragons which were plump and either comically fierce or warmly friendly, with humanly expressive faces. There was no sign of anything with the flavour of her dream —the flavour of primeval, mindless destruction. . . . She looked carefully along the shelf. No more dragons at all. She glanced round the room—Fiction— Non-Fiction—where did you look?

A little reluctantly, she approached the young librarian, whose knees jutted painfully above the edge of the low table she had chosen. "Sorry to interrupt," said Jen to the librarian, "but have you any books on dragons—other than the stories over there?" The two little girls were propped forward on to the table on their forearms, kneeling up on their chairs, and pretending to look at the page from which she read. The small boy still drummed, quite contentedly, and prattled on, unheeded but at least unchecked. "I seen a monster," he was saying, as Jen drew near. "I seen a monster crawling in the dark. It's got a big sharp sting and it can sting you all dead."

"No, I'm afraid not," said the librarian. "You could try the books on Chinese Art in the main Library."

All through her words came the imperturbable piping of the small gypsy boy. "I seen a dragon last night. It got millions and millions and millions of legs."

"Thank you," said Jen, and turned for the general shelves. Part way across the room she glanced back, but the scene was much as before, the librarian ploughing on with her task and ignoring, as people usually do, the piping fantasies of the youngest of her charges.

The book which looked as though it would be the most useful one was among the extra large books on a bottom shelf. Jen squatted on her haunches with the heavy book propped uncomfortably on her knees and turned the pages. Chinese dragons passed before her

55

eyes—cloud-like dragons, ferocious dragons, pairs of dragons playing with, or perhaps trying to capture, the sacred pearl—dragons roaring round dishes—drifting across plates—crouching as handles at the edges of urns —all of them a little like her dream, yet not really like, not truly like, nothing that she could identify with any certainty. Then came paper dragons—dragon kites—the dragon boat festival—an enormous dragon structure which was carried through the streets over the heads and shoulders of maybe a dozen men, so that their legs were its legs.

"It got millions and millions and millions of legs."

She stared at that one for a long time. It wasn't right, though. It wasn't scaly; its tail, although long, was blunt. Impossible to imagine the dream thing without the accompanying sharpness.

But there was something else about the picture which caught her attention. A man stood at the front of this carnival dragon, and at first Jen had assumed that he was pretending to hold its head, that when the time came he would lead it through the crowds as you might lead a real beast. But actually now that she looked again she saw that he wasn't holding its head at all, he was doing something to its eye. He had a paintbrush in his raised hand, a minute pot hanging by his side from the other hand. He was painting an eye in place on the ferocious mask.

She glanced down at the caption.

"The ceremony of dotting the eye of the dragon," she read. "When the eye has been marked in place the dragon is officially 'alive'."

Jen's feet and ankles were tingling with pins and needles and she sat down, hard, on the floor.

"I seen a monster crawling in the dark. It's got a big sharp sting and it can sting you all dead."

Small children fantasize all the time. They're not lying when they say they've seen witches and goblins and monsters—in a way, they don't expect to be believed literally. She knew he had picked up the idea of a dragon from what she had said—but it was the way he talked about it that disturbed her. Crawling, he'd said. It did seem to crawl, the dream thing, although she had an odd feeling that it could rear up like a bear if it wanted to. And what had made him talk about a sharp sting? That wasn't a particularly usual attribute of a nightmare.

She closed the book on the photograph of the Chinese, heedlessly bringing his creation to life, put it back in its shelf and stood up. "They've built it in my head," she thought. "And now I've set it free. And it's hunting."

Her feelings about the gypsies had become so complex that she had hoped to be able to ignore everything to do with them until she was able to think things out calmly—but now she stood alone in an empty corner of the Library and fear began to hit her and withdraw rhythmically, like sea waves. First a rush of fear that made her feel dizzy, then a sickening dragging feeling in her stomach and inside her bones as it drew back from her before the next onslaught—over and over again. The original hatred had changed into fear, but the embryonic beginnings of a new kind of hate were there, too, caused by the fear and by a sense of injustice that they should be doing all this to her. So irrational did this fear make her that she lost all urge to understand the creature and for a few moments almost believed that she could make them leave the land under the flyover by sheer force of wishing.

But then she began to think more clearly—or at least in words that made some sense to her. She thought about the hundred-year-old bequest which the council dared not look into for fear. . . .

She went up to the desk at the corner of the Lending Library.

"Excuse me," she said. "Do you have anything in here about Benjamin Spicer?"

The librarian gave her a slightly odd look, she thought, but made no comment. Just said, "You mean Benjamin Spencer? Local man, born . . ."

"Yes," said Jen. "Him."

"There's one small book," said the librarian, sidling out from behind her counter and heading for a short shelf entitled 'Local History.' "A biography, privately published in a limited edition by his son in 1891." She took it from its place—a short, slim volume bound in dingy green. Old, but not well thumbed.

"Thank you," said Jen.

She leant her shoulder on the shelf and turned the pages where she stood. He had led a dull but worthy life, Benjamin Spencer, spending such wealth as he had for the good of the community. The 'common land' had not, in fact, been left in his will but had been given to the town, or rather to its people, as a gift during his lifetime, to be held by them in perpetuity 'for the pleasure, use and recreation of the residents'. . . .

Jen wasn't sure whether or not the massive stone legs of the flyover interfered with the pleasure and recreation of the residents, but surely anyone could see that the presence of the gypsy camp did; if only because there was no room for anyone else on the land so long as they were there.

She found a clean paper hanky in her pocket, tore off a long strip, and laid it carefully in the relevant page, so that it hung out at each end. She knew now what she was going to do. She was going to take the book to Tom's parents. There was something slightly ignoble about the plan that made her uneasy, but then she, having found the information, had no idea how to make use of it, or even if it was useful.

She carried the book up to the desk. "I'll take this, please," she said.

When she had stamped it the librarian moved as if to withdraw the strip of tissue, thinking it had been left by some past borrower.

"No, that's my marker," said Jen. "That's important."

She cut through the Children's Library on her way to the main exit. But the gypsy children were being collected by their father, the tall red-faced man with the hay-like hair. And the little boys' unceasing voice was now concerned with the story he had just been read. Jen walked quickly past behind them and out into the street. They didn't see her go.

# 9

SHE KNEW SHE was being followed as soon as she turned the corner from the Library into the long quiet street that led towards Tom's home. It wasn't that she could hear anything, other than the sound of her own footsteps, it was rather that she could sense someone behind her just as you can sense when someone is watching you.

The thought came into her mind almost at once that it might be the tall gypsy, although she wasn't sure why she thought he should follow her, or for what purpose. And if it was him, he must have sent his children back to the camp on their own because it was inconceivable that that small boy could keep quiet for more than a minute at a time.

Jen began to walk a little faster. The way from the Library to Tom's home was along side or back roads which were lined with small, semi-detached houses, broken by the odd patch of terrace, and with trees growing at intervals from the pavement edge. She had never known these roads to be anything but quiet and un-frightening. But, in a way, that became the very prob-lem—they were so quiet—you hardly ever saw people going in or out of their houses, few cars passed and the street lights were just a little too far apart.

She was about half way down the road when it occurred to her to cross over. There was no need to cross because the road turned sharp left at the end, and she wanted to turn sharp left with it, but it struck her as rather a good way of finding out if whoever was behind was actually following or just happening to walk in the same direction. She would cross, and if he crossed too, she would cross immediately back. If he was quite innocent he would stay on the other side and go into one of the houses. But if he followed her across *and* back . . .

Her main hope was that he would turn out to be some perfectly normal person going home. If she proved to herself that he was trailing her, she wasn't quite sure what she would do about it.

She moved to the edge of the kerb and although her ears told her there was no traffic at all, she glanced quite automatically to the right before stepping off. She saw the whole road and both pavements stretching right back to the corner where the lights of the Library blazed out. There was no one there. Road and pavements were quite empty.

Intensely relieved, Jen didn't bother to cross, but continued to walk on the same side, her hand resting on the book that was stretching her coat pocket.

But she hadn't passed more than three or four houses before the sense of being followed began slowly to seep back into her mind. Knowing that there was nobody there, she refused to allow herself to look back.

It's very easy to get spooked, she thought conversationally to herself, and once I give in to it and start to look over my shoulder it'll just get worse and worse. I'll end up walking backwards.

To take her mind off it she began to look more carefully at the houses she was passing. A few showed comforting chinks of light between their curtains in their downstairs rooms. One wonderful house had its lights on and curtains back so that she could see the blue flicker of the television set, the wall-to-ceiling bookshelves, and two armchairs with the tops of heads just showing over their backs. Several ground floors were invisible behind hedges. But most were dark and empty. Although the black winter sky made it plain that it was night-time, it was still early and people who went out to work were not yet home.

There was someone behind her. She knew it by the back of her neck and by her spine. Without planning to, she looked quickly round over her shoulder.

The street was empty.

As she turned back she felt a tiny sharp twinge in her shoulder. I'll get a stiff neck if I go on like this, she thought.

She reached the left turn and took it, crossed the road and turned right, all the time trying to work out in her mind if there was any way she could get to Tom's by busier roads. But there wasn't. Not without walking along three sides of a square. In fact she would spend more time walking along back roads to and from the main road than she would take to walk directly to Tom's along the roads she was already on.

She walked on, trying to keep a steady pace, hearing the regular clump, clump of her own footsteps, looking into the dark houses she passed, ignoring the warning tinglings in the back of her neck, dreading the pools of darkness when she was exactly between two lamp posts, relieved to watch the next lamp post growing steadily nearer to her.

But as she drew level with the next lamp post she saw, out of the corner of her eye, a huge shadow grow on the pavement behind her to her left, and then swing silently round beside her.

She heard the harsh intake of her own breath as she spun round to face the follower who had closed in so soundlessly.

There was no one there.

The shadow was her own, sliding past her on her left as she passed the street lamp on her right.

She leant back against the nearest garden wall, her head against the bristly hedge and her palms against the rough cold brick, and waited while her breathing steadied and her heart stopped pounding the whole road into rhythmic movement.

She had been too badly frightened even to feel silly, and somehow her own hiss of fright echoed in her memory and made everything worse. The hedge began to prick the back of her neck and she moved away from the wall. She had a sharp stitch in her side, although she hadn't been running, and a tiny sharp pain in the middle of her left calf. There was still, even now that she was looking up and down a completely deserted road, the feeling of someone there, of being watched, of being the centre of attention. But the houses were empty, so there was no point in knocking on someone's door—and if they hadn't been empty, would she have knocked? What could she say? What was there to do but walk on? Walk on faster, with now a tiny sharp pain in her knee and now one in the palm of her hand.

It was the little sharp twinges, so brief but so persistent, that confirmed in her mind the growing picture she had of what might be following her.

She walked on and now she did look round, often, not knowing whether or not she expected to see anything, not knowing whether in fact it was visible.

There was no one in the road and no car passed. It seemed that she was the only human being abroad.

She wasn't even sure, any more, if she felt she was being watched from behind, or if it was from one side, or to the front.

She approached the gap between two pairs of semi-detached houses. The deep darkness caught in this gap was suddenly filled with menace.

She walked a little more quickly. Stared ahead. Didn't want to run because it was too far to run all the way to Tom's.

She drew level with the gap. Didn't want to look into it. But did look, as she hurried past. The darkness was too thick to see anything at all. Something that she couldn't see lay huge and heavy against the house wall.

She hurried past, turned another corner, began on another empty residential street, all the time drawing closer to Tom's, all the time thinking just let me get there, don't close in out here.

There were scratches on the garden walls, visible in the dim orange street lighting. Scratches which sometimes carried on right across gates. Perhaps they were always there.

Whether or not they were always there, they began to assume huge significance.

The black gaps between houses became awe-full, fear-full. Something moved along with her; now behind, now beside, now ahead, dragging something hard and sharp across surfaces; rising up invisible in the darkest places as if it would scale the houses and slide down far walls to keep pace; never seen, never even glimpsed, but seeing, watching, through that one, tiny dot.

Along roads which she hardly saw now, past houses, black gaps, scarred walls, silences that listened, scraped lamp posts, blind darkness that watched, walking faster, breathing faster, heart beating fit to disturb whole streets, running a little, running faster, running in the centre of its eye, running to the gate she knew, up the path she knew, knocking on the door she knew.

And then meek, breathless, letting herself be ushered firmly into the sitting room, so brightly lit, so very warm, Mr and Mrs Welsh aware of no problem, calling Tom down from his room, Tom coming, friendly but abstracted and bringing the book he was half way through, Fred following, half asleep.

Tom sitting by the fire, reading out odd bits from *Black Elk Speaks,* Fred dreaming and twitching across his shoes, Tom's parents sitting in their usual places, his mother listening, his father offering suitable remarks like 'Those Yanks have got a lot to answer for', and 'Shameful way to treat a noble race'. Jen, safe, half listening, half trying to forget about the book she had left, unnoticed, on the hall table.

"No, thank you," she said when offered coffee or tea. She didn't want anyone to go out of the room while she was there and see the book where it lay. She wouldn't entertain the thought that, even if they found it after she'd gone, they'd guess who had left it there. In some way she felt that if she could shut her own mind to what she'd done, no one else could know, either. She almost believed, as she sat there, that she hadn't done anything at all. The book existed in this world, and so did the Welshs' need to know what was in it. Now the book and the Welshs were in the same house together, and what happened next had nothing to do with her.

Then Mr Welsh struggled to his feet, muttered something, the way people do when they're going to the lavatory, and went out of the room.

"I must be going now," said Jen, and stood up. Something pressed more closely against the windows, behind their neatly drawn curtains.

"Wait a moment," said Mrs Welsh briskly, "and Mr Welsh will run you home. You shouldn't be wandering about on your own so late."

Normally Jen would have refused the offer, even quite curtly. She was irritated by the picture they somehow always painted of a feeble-minded female drifting vaguely about in the night and inviting danger from every quarter. But this night she said, "Thank you, that would be nice."

And wondered why, since it seemed to have no actual substance, the dream thing was kept at bay by bricks and mortar and panes of glass. She had no sooner thought that than it began to seep slowly into the room from under the curtains.

She was still standing, and she swung round to face it, although there was nothing to see, just the sensation of something enormous sliding scale by scale, leg by leg, into the room, the eye of its attention focused sharply on her.

Mr Welsh came back through the door, quite slowly. He was carrying the book. He was half reading the book, looking at the page where the marker hung. "Look at this," he was saying, half to himself. "This is interesting."

He was clearly unaware of the slow and awful invasion.

He crossed to his wife and handed the book to her. He squatted down on his haunches beside her chair and his knee caps cracked loudly. He pointed to the part he wanted her to read.

"Where did this come from?" said Mrs Welsh.

"It was on the hall table," said Mr Welsh. And then, to Jen, "Is it yours?"

Jen didn't answer.

Tom's attention was drawn out of his own book. "What is it?" he said, looking round the faces which were all turned away from him, his parents still intent on the little green book, Jen still staring at the window.

Tom got up and moved across to read over his mother's shoulder, leaning on the back of her armchair and moving her hair with his breath.

He didn't read for long. He wandered slowly towards Jen and stopped a little way from her. "Ammunition for the Residents' Association, is it?" he said quietly.

Jen looked at him. Most of her mind was numbed with the thought that it was about to be engulfed by something appalling—only a small portion of it was able to register the expression on Tom's face.

Still she said nothing.

"How do you feel about Jews?" said Tom, conversationally. "And blacks?"

A spark of its own life flickered across Jen's brain. "That's a disgusting thing to say," she hissed at him.

"You share the Führer's views on gypsies," said Tom, with a distaste so deep that there was no passion in his voice at all. "I wondered if you shared his views on Jews as well?"

At that moment the last section of the dream thing insinuated its invisible way into the room.

This is my imagination, Jen thought. No one else is aware of anything. There isn't anything there. This is pure imagination—I must control it.

And Fred the passive began to growl.

Even Tom was startled. "I've never heard him growl before," he said.

Jen turned to look at Fred. Was he simply confirming its presence, or might he, oh blessed dog, be able to see it off?

But Fred was not growling at the full empty space in front of the window. Fred was growling at her.

# 10

"I HOPE YOU thanked him for driving you home?"

"Yes."

"Has he made you feel car sick or something?"

"No. Why?"

"Well, are you still subdued because of last night?"

"Don't be cross," said Jen, "but I just don't want to think about last night at all—not yet."

"All right," said her mother, without looking round. She was watching over a panful of boiling spaghetti, every now and then drawing a long thread of it up on a fork and nipping off the end to test if it was cooked. A pot of savoury sauce bubbled beside the spaghetti pan. Then, "This is ready. Put some forks and mats on the table, would you?"

"Don't give me much," said Jen, getting out the cork mats. "I don't really want any."

"You can't give up sleeping *and* eating."

Jen didn't answer. She felt more tired than she could ever remember having felt in all her life. Not sleepy, and not really physically tired, either, although she felt that she would like to go and lie on her bed for about a week without moving. This was a different sort of tiredness and it meant that she couldn't be bothered to think, or talk, or respond to anything. She felt as though all her energies had been drained out of her—but she also felt that they had been replaced by something else, perhaps because nature abhors a vacuum. They had been replaced by a thick and heavy fog which filled her head and her limbs so completely that they ached a little with the pressure.

Her mother reached across the table to put a plate, not too full, in front of her.

"There's more if you want it," she said.

"Thanks," said Jen. The effort to get the word out was almost too much. She stared at the food and realised that she probably wasn't going to be able to summon up enough energy to use the fork. She made herself pick the fork up, and it seemed as heavy as a garden spade.

Her brain was too sluggish to register a very strong emotion, but, in among the fog, strands of fear began to appear.

"What's the matter?" said her mother, who had already eaten half a plateful. "Don't you like it?"

"I'm so tired," said Jen. "Can't be bothered."

"I'm not surprised. You've had two bad nights and you've been so strung up lately I think it's amazing you've got enough energy left in you to sit upright."

Jen looked across at her, surprised. "Feel full of lead," she said. "Fork's too heavy."

"Do you think I've never felt like that? Some Friday nights I can hardly be bothered to speak. Life is often tiring, Jen, you'll have to accept that."

"Haven't done enough to be this tired."

"You have. Growing's tiring. Not sleeping is tiring.

Not eating is tiring. Getting into a state, whatever it's about, is tiring."

"I feel," said Jen, just in case her mother didn't realise how all embracing this tiredness was, "that I'm full up with it—that I need to go and lie down, for a long time, and let it kind of seep out of me."

"Well, you do," said her mother calmly. "And it will. Try and shovel some food in if you can, because that'll help, and then go straight to bed."

Jen scraped up a forkful of sauce. Most of it ran off again, but she ate what was left.

"And I'll be all right tomorrow?" she said.

"No. You'll still feel tired tomorrow. But if you have another early night you'll probably be all right the next day. If you feel really grim you can stay home tomorrow if you like. Have a headache."

"*Can* I?"

"Yes. We'll decide now that you're not going in, if you like. Then you can sleep late. But Jen, you must promise to try and calm down a bit. You have to learn how to do it, you know. You can't go on living at such a pitch of tension and anger. You'll wear yourself out completely and make yourself ill."

"I'll try. I really can't eat this."

"All right. Have a glass of milk. And try to think about nice things, or at least neutral things, for a while."

The knock on the door made them both jump. Mrs Herratt let herself in and trotted through into the kitchen.

"Oh dear, I'm interrupting your tea," she said. She was carrying a bottle of milk stout and a packet of crisps.

"It's all right," said Jen's mother wearily, getting up and picking up the plates. "We've finished. Jen, get a glass of milk and an apple, will you?"

71

"I've just popped out to the Off Licence so I've got some change and I can give you back that phone money you lent me," said Mrs Herratt, putting two coins down on the fridge top with a flourish. "I don't like to be in debt."

"Thank you. There was no rush."

"Ooh, there's going to be some bother about that lot under the flyover," said Mrs Herratt with relish. "Never mind not being able to move them on, the police'll be arresting them soon, I shouldn't wonder."

Jen poured out a glass of milk and looked at her mother—who put the dishes into the sink and turned the jet of hot water on to them without comment.

Mrs Herratt had moved aside to let Jen get at the fridge. Now she moved back again and leant comfortably against it, hugging her bag and bottle to her fit to crush the crisps.

"All this thieving and damage there's been," she said. "Have you heard?"

"No," said Jen's mother.

"Oh, I thought you'd have picked up all the gossip from the customers in your little boutique. They're all talking about it in the greengrocer's. But then, I suppose your customers are a bit too grand to be interested in everyday matters. There's been all kinds of little thefts in the streets all around there, you know. Car radios gone, and things from garden sheds, and they've even been in some of the houses. Course they didn't get much—there isn't much to get around here—but they've had one or two tellys, odd bits of money, the rent money from the teapot, that kind of thing."

"It always happens," said Jen's mother, scrubbing out the inside of the saucepan. "Whenever 'gypsies' come into an area the local petty thieves get to work. They know exactly who'll be blamed."

"I haven't heard *that* one before," said Mrs Herratt, momentarily taken aback.

"It's quite usual, I assure you."

Mrs Herratt recovered her attitudes. "Well, dear, even supposing you're right," she said, "them gypsies are still the cause of all the thieving, aren't they? We'd still be better off if they weren't there, wouldn't we? And what about all the destruction—plants torn up in front gardens, damage to parked cars . . . "

"What kind of damage?" said Jen, with a memory of the scarred surfaces that seemed to mark the passage of the creature.

"Oh, scratches mostly. Great lines scraped out of the paintwork."

"Kids," said Jen's mother.

"Gypsy kids," said Mrs Herratt. "Mind, they're not without their share of trouble, too. Him in the Off Licence says one of the caravans was damaged this very evening. Looks as if someone tried to turn it over, he says. The sides are all bashed in. People won't stand for it, you see."

"For what!"

"For them *being* there, causing all this bother . . . "

"Mrs Herratt," said Jen, "when was the trailer damaged?"

"This evening, dear. About five, I think he said. They'll have waited till it got dark, you see."

Jen turned away from her and wandered over to the window. She half heard Mrs Herratt saying, "You won't see anything from here, dear," and her mother interrupting her with some quite different comment.

She ignored them both and leant with her hands on the windowsill, staring at her own face reflected darkly back at her against the night beyond the glass. Her eyes looked exceptionally round and moist, like a seal's eyes.

At about five o'clock she had been standing in the Library, buffeted by waves of fear and half believing in her own power to move the encampment by sheer force of wishing. She stared into the luminous eyes of the dark other-self in the window. Was it at all possible that, having released their creation, she now had some power over it—was it possible that in her hatred and fear she had turned their own weird hound back on to them?

". . . a taboo subject," her mother was saying, behind her. "We know we disagree about the travellers, Mrs Herratt, and there's no point in our having an argument about it. Neither of us is ever going to change the views of the other — and we are neighbours . . . "

. Jen carried the glass of milk and the apple through into her own room and stood them on the dressing table. They echoed back at her out of the mirror, like an advertisement for healthy living.

But it's *their* creature, she thought. And even though I wished them gone I didn't wish damage on them or their property. But then who in history had ever succeeded in creating a monster and controlling it completely—didn't it always wreak general havoc as well as obeying specific commands. . . ?

Anyhow, none of this business must be allowed to matter. She had already taken practical steps to help the Residents' Association—it was up to them now to take further practical steps. If she did have any ability to deflect its power, then she would use it if ever it closed in again. In the meantime, no more was required of her at all.

She decided to switch her mind off the whole situation—block it out—sleep by night and think neutral thoughts, as her mother had said, by day, until the gypsies went, taking their monster with them. Let the others engineer the eviction whenever they felt able to act.

They felt able, as it happened, to act very fast.

"You-know-who are leaving tomorrow," said Melanie, in a hoarse whisper, leaning right on to Jen's desk and cupping her hands round her mouth to direct her words straight down Jen's ear.

"How do you know?" said Jen, in her normal voice since the hubbub in the early morning classroom made whispering seem rather unnecessary.

"My dad said, last night," hissed Melanie. "You'll feel better then, won't you?"

Jen shrugged. "It's not important."

"Oh but *I* know it is," said Melanie, and clasped her hand comfortingly over Jen's forearm. "*I* know how awful all this has been for you. Has *he* said any more?"

"Who?" said Jen, knowing who.

"*You* know. *Him*." She arched her neck slightly so that she pointed with the top of her head towards Tom, two rows away.

"Oh, I forget if he has or not," said Jen. The exaggerated kindness in the hand made her arm itch and she drew it away as gently as she could. "It doesn't matter. Specially if they're going."

"Oh yes," said Melanie. "My dad says good always triumphs in the end. He's one of the people that's making them go."

"Probably they were going anyway," said Jen. "They do tend to move around."

"Oh no. They weren't. They said they wouldn't. But if they don't go tomorrow, early, they're going to be towed away. The police are going to be there and everything."

"The police!"

"In case they turn nasty," said Melanie with relish.

"I expect they'll just go," said Jen. "They like to move about. They must be sick of that rotten flyover. I expect they'll be glad to go." She was relieved, but something felt uncomfortable in her, a shoes-on-the-wrong-feet feeling.

"Yes," said Melanie. "And then *he'll* forget they were ever there. You'll see. He'll be friendly again, like before."

"I wish you'd use people's names," said Jen snappishly. "Why don't you?"

Melanie gave her a wounded look. "I just wanted you to know," she said, "that your true friends don't think any the less of you because *they* came here."

"Yes," said Jen. "Good. Thank you. Can I copy your French? I haven't done mine. I'll put in some mistakes."

# 11

IT WAS VERY bright and clear and cold—the coldest day of the autumn so far. The site looked cleaner in the early morning light than she had remembered it, less squalid. The heap of junk that the gypsies seemed to have accumulated was stacked up against one of the legs of the flyover, to the back of the site, and the trailers and vehicles stood forming a pattern, a very wide semi-circle, with the goats at the far end.

The goats were restive, put on edge by the extra people on the site and perhaps by the sense of impending activity that hung over it.

The police were very much in evidence, although they weren't doing anything. Three police cars were parked on the slip road from the motorway to the site. The men from the front car had got out and were standing at its offside, leaning on the roof and calmly watching developments. The occupants of the other two cars remained in their seats, but even from her position on the far side of the great road Jen could see that their heads were turned away from her, towards the gypsies.

In front of the leading police car, and just at the junction of slip road and main road, the big council towing vehicle stood. The driver and his mate sat inside, out of the cold, waiting, presumably, for a signal to hitch up to the nearest caravan. The early morning traffic was sparse and offered no hindrance.

On the site itself the big, fair man faced a man in a raincoat and a tall policeman who looked to Jen to be quite senior. Behind him and to his right the old woman smoked her briar on the steps of her home, but no one else was to be seen. At least not at first. As Jen watched, and her eyes grew accustomed to focusing on the distance, she realised that there was a group of faces in every window—the small faces of the children low down at the corners, the larger adult faces in the middle.

One or two other early risers, passing Jen on the pavement, slowed down a little, staring over at the encampment which looked so different now that the police were there—but as the scene remained peculiarly static they went on their way.

Jen's hands, in their gloves, were pushed so deeply into the pockets of her coat that the front of it dipped down into two points. It was very cold, although there wasn't much wind. Mostly she was conscious of the cold on her cheekbones and the soles of her feet, through her shoes.

Nobody else had come out to watch the eviction, which struck her as odd. They had engineered it, she and the Residents' Association, and she had expected to see them, and to see Tom, and to watch the gypsies go and the site become wholesome once more, and to be able to persuade Tom to admit that it was better without them; and that they were better off wherever they had gone. But on the other hand, perhaps the less Tom saw of the gypsies, going or staying, the sooner he would forget. And what exactly would he say to her at this moment, knowing as he did that she had supplied the ammunition for the imminent rout? The others, though, they should have come. It seemed cowardly to set a chain of events in motion and then hide while someone else got on with the difficult bits.

Cowardly, too, to stand on the far side of the road, no more involved than if she had been watching on television at home. Jen walked over to the opening of the dank underpass and crossed beneath the road to the goat-guarded exit.

She felt a little braver about passing the goats with the police so near at hand. The one nearest to her lowered its head, as if it thought it was a billy-goat, but she kept out of range and it could do no more.

Viewing the scene from the other side now, she saw a policeman she had not noticed before, standing half behind a caravan. He saw her in the same moment and began to walk towards her, everything about his slow movements and expression telling her that he was going to shoo her away. Then the scene behind him changed and he stopped to look round.

The big, fair man detached himself from the tiny group and climbed into his home, slamming the door behind him. At once the man in the raincoat stepped forward and banged on the door. The policeman who had been approaching Jen made a dismissing gesture at her with his arm and wandered back to watch. The raincoated man banged again. Jen moved closer, behind the broad back of the second policeman. She was very frightened—frightened still of the goats behind her, frightened of the gypsies, frightened even of disobeying the policeman—but she wanted to be truly present, to claim responsibility for her part.

The dropping of that book on the hall table without comment was the action that tasted bad—small and mean. Walking in and handing them the book, risking Tom's comments and theirs, would have been different, all right. But it could be retrieved if she stepped forward now. Confessing always made things all right. Owning up always neutralised uncomfortable feelings.

The door of the caravan opened quite suddenly and the fair-haired man came out again. The man in the raincoat stepped smartly back and trod into the senior policeman. One or two other people were coming out of their caravans now.

Jen had sidled up until she was level with the blue caravan, next to the fair man's. It was the one whose side had been buckled in. She looked at the damaged metal and then something made her glance up. Two little bright-eyed children were staring at her out of the window. She looked back at them, but they didn't shift their eyes, just stared as small children do, their heads framed in the chintz curtains.

"She's not ready to move," said the fair-haired gypsy. He was facing his enemies, but there was something so unexpected about his attitude that Jen could not at first define it. She had thought he might be afraid, or indignant, or angry. But, despite the bright invigorating morning, despite the faint aura of menace that drifted over the scene, he was bored, deeply bored.

The man in the raincoat was bored, too. He drew a deep sigh and said what he had obviously said before. "You're illegally parked here. The order to move you on has come through. I must ask you to leave right away."

Jen leant her shoulder against the battered caravan,

below the perky heads in the window. She stood, huddled down into her coat. No one took any notice of her.

"We've been moved on six times in the last five weeks," said the gypsy. "She's tired."

"You're being offered places on a council site. When you're settled in there nobody will move you on any more."

"And suppose we want to move?"

"You've just said that you're tired of moving."

"I want to go when I want to go. At the council site won't the trailers be fixed to the ground?"

"They will."

"What's the use in that? Can we graze the goats?"

"No livestock."

"Is there somewhere to put the scrap?"

"It's a caravan site, not a tip."

"What am I supposed to live on?"

"Social Security doesn't let people starve."

"I work for my living, like you."

"Oh yes? What's your trade, then?"

"I deal in scrap. That 'tip' there—that's worth money. It took labour to get it there. Now you say I have to leave it and move on—for the seventh time in five weeks."

"You haven't the right to stay. The land belongs to the town, and the town doesn't want you here."

"Do you think I don't know that? This isn't a good place for us—there's more hatred here than we've met in years."

"Are you saying you've been threatened?"

"Not like you mean. But hatred itself is a threat."

The man in the raincoat looked at his watch. "Are you going to go?" he said.

"No. The baby is two days old and she needs to rest with him."

"All right." He turned and moved away, raising his arm in a weary signal. The two policemen followed him at a distance that was discreet rather than respectful. They were keeping a low profile. The engine of the towing truck droned into action. The gypsy stood where he was.

Jen cowered slightly against the blue caravan, leaning into its damaged side. Why did the gypsy talk as if the hatred was a danger to them, when they'd started it, created it?

People were coming out of their vans now, to watch. They stood, they leant, they didn't say much to one another. One or two looked over at Jen—and when a woman, closely followed by two little boys, came out of the caravan Jen was actually leaning against, she looked at her quite closely with a puzzled expression—but Jen looked away and neither of them spoke.

On the steps of the far caravan a little girl sat at the feet of the old woman. In her hands she held one end of a length of thick string—at the other end of the string, and half under the steps of the caravan, the little yellow puppy foraged busily.

Slowly, slowly, the heavy towing vehicle reversed across the littered grass. The tall gypsy stood still outside his caravan and watched as it approached him. It lurched on until it was about two feet from him. Then it stopped. He made no sign that he would have moved if it had not stopped. He watched unemotionally as the driver got out and walked back along the vehicle towards him. And Jen saw something else. He was not just bored—he was tired, bone-tired with working and moving and worrying.

The driver stopped to detach one end of the cable from

the back of the vehicle, which stood juddering, its engine still running. When he straightened up he found himself almost face to face with the gypsy.

"Sorry, mate," he said automatically. "Nothing to do with me." And moved as if to attach the cable to the tow-bar of the caravan.

The gypsy moved very slightly to block his path. They were so close to each other that he had to do little more than shift his weight from one foot to the other. "What do you mean," he said, "nothing to do with you?"

"Nothing personal," said the other man, raising his voice above the noise of the engine, "but I got to shift you first, they say."

"We want to stay here one week," said the gypsy.

"I got to shift you now." He edged past, crouched down, attached the cable, straightened up, dusted his hands on his dungarees, elaborately casual, aware of all the eyes upon him.

Watching him, Jen thought, "I understand how you feel. You're like me. You have to do what's right even when it isn't pleasant. We'll get rid of them together, you and me."

"It's not good to move on a Friday," said the gypsy. "We never move on a Friday."

"Nor on any other day of the week neither, I suppose," said the driver.

He was beginning to turn away, towards the driver's cab of the vehicle. The group of people stood quietly, except for one small girl who hopped from foot to foot in a gawky little dance of her own invention. The police leant on their cars and watched. Jen thought, Soon. Soon all the nastiness will be over.

But then the gypsy lay down on the grass, quite

undramatically, half across the towing cable, and in front of the wheels of his own caravan.

For a moment the other man stood rigidly, staring at him. Then he moved towards him and held out a hand as if to help him up. "Oh look, be fair, mate," he said. "I got to do my job."

Two policemen pushed themselves away from their car and began to move in slowly.

"Why?" said the gypsy from the ground.

"Because I have. I got my orders. This is something for the authorities to decide, not you or me."

"I have decided," said the gypsy. "I've decided to stay. She had the baby two nights ago and she's wore out. And you've decided. You've decided to move us, even though you'll probably kill her."

"I haven't decided *nothing*," said the driver desperately. "I'm just obeying orders. You can't do no good down there—here comes the fuzz—they'll just shift you."

The first policeman cast his shadow across both men. "Come on now. Get up," he said.

Unexpectedly, the gypsy jumped to his feet, but he ignored the policeman. His eyes were fixed on the man in front of him. "You don't believe me," he said. "You want to see?" And turned and went into his home.

He came out again almost immediately, a woman's voice calling softly from behind him. "It's all right," he said over his shoulder. "I'll not be long."

In his arms he held a smallish bundle of red cloth. He pulled part of it aside.

Even from where she stood Jen could see the tiny face, grimacing in the bright light, and the minute fist that reached upwards, fragile and un-co-ordinated. She

84

swayed forward, instinctively wanting to cover the baby and protect it from the cold, hard morning.

Before she could forget herself further, the driver took three quick steps and tweaked the covering back over the baby's arm. "It's too cold for him outside," he said. "Take him back in."

Without a word the gypsy turned and disappeared inside.

The two policemen stood still. From the far side of the site the raincoated man approached, calling, "What's the trouble?" across the distance.

No one answered him.

Jen stared at the caravan and tried to visualise the woman inside reaching out her arms for her baby, making him warm again after his shocking exposure. He was going to grow up into someone very much like the little boy who had drummed his feet in the library, and whom she could pick out in a group of three children near the old woman's caravan; would grow up to talk about dragons and danger and to be hated and moved on—that is, if he survived the present eviction.

In her mind she saw Mrs Herratt's gloating face and Mrs Welsh's pinched and mean one—saw Tom's expression of distaste—and heard her mother say, "Have you noticed what nice company you and your opinions keep?"

But I *must* be right, she thought. The police are on my side. . . .

The group had re-formed. The driver's mate, who had been sticking his head enquiringly out of the cab of the vehicle at regular intervals, had shut off the engine and joined the driver at the rear. The man in the raincoat was flanked by the two silent policemen. The senior police officer was strolling up from his distance. The gypsy stood outside his door.

"You're paid to do a job," said the man in the raincoat.

"Try sacking me, then, and see what the union says," said the driver. "I'm not having anything to do with it."

"These people are not supposed to *be* here."

"Well I can't see what harm they're doing. And I'm not going to shake up that baby in there—he's no bigger than a tadpole."

"We'll go in one week," said the gypsy. "Under our own power."

The senior policeman joined the group discreetly.

"To the council site?" asked the man in the raincoat.

"No."

"Then where?"

"None of your business. You want us off, we'll get off. Somewhere else."

"All right," said the man in the raincoat as if he had won the battle rather than lost it. "I'll give you one week, to the hour, and if you're not off . . ."

"We'll be off."

"If you're not off," said the senior policeman, taking up the line, "I can't guarantee your safety."

"That a threat?" said the gypsy.

"No. A fact. There are people in this town ready to form a private army to get you out."

"That won't be the first time," said the gypsy.

"If they think we can't get rid of you," the policeman persisted, "they'll take over. We can't always be around. If they get to you before my men know about it, we can't be held responsible for what may happen. Understand?"

"Good day to you," said the gypsy.

Jen watched them go. These were her people, who

were retreating in a kind of defeat, and yet quite a large part of her felt relieved that the encampment had been saved for seven days—seven days to rest, and to build up the baby for his journey.

She watched the big council vehicle bumping off the grass and on to the road; watched as the police cars left, one by one; and suddenly realised that she was alone, in the middle of the encampment, and that attention, freed from the other intruders, was now focusing on her.

She had come to confess and hadn't said a word. And so had almost forgotten her own presence. She stood up straight and walked quickly across to the tall gypsy. He had turned to go back indoors but was being hampered by the small boy who suddenly bounced over and seized him by one hand, leaning back with all his slight weight, just for the pleasure of something to swing on.

"Excuse me," said Jen.

The man turned and looked down at her with a slightly preoccupied expression on his face. Then, "I've seen you before," he said.

Jen thought, I must remember that I *am* right. The police are on my side. Most of the town's on my side. Aloud she said, "I came here before—to ask you to go away."

All that she was aware of now was his face, red and weather-marked, and his eyes looking into hers. The earlier strange hush had left the site, freeing the sounds of traffic, the shrieks of children starting to play, the discussing voices of people and the odd bark from dogs newly released from the battered truck. These sounds came and went in her ears, but didn't seem to relate to her.

An expression came on to his tired face, but Jen wasn't

sure what it was. It crossed her mind that he might be going to hit her and she took half a step back before she knew for certain that he would never do that.

"I remember," he said. "So you came to watch us moved on, did you? Disappointed now, I hope."

"I want to explain something to you," said Jen.

The man stood looking down at her, rocking slightly as the little boy pulled unconcernedly on his wrist. He said nothing.

"They didn't know, right away, that you weren't allowed to camp here," said Jen. "I found out and I told them. I want you to know that."

She didn't know what she had expected from him, but she hadn't expected him to look puzzled. "Are you trying to say you're sorry?" he said.

"No—no, I think I did right. But I want you to know, because if you *don't* know then it means I just—kind of—told tales on you. Do you see? And it wasn't like that. And I had to do something to get rid of you."

The puzzlement went. He looked as though he understood something, and was not impressed. "There's something else you want to be rid of," he said. "Not us."

"What do you mean?"

He stared at her with eyes that seemed to see right into her brain. For a short, fanciful moment she half thought that she felt the dream thing move inside her head and stare back at him.

"You're starting young, aren't you?" he said. "What do you want me to say to you? Do you want me to shout at you? Will you feel less guilty if I get angry with you? I don't have time for spiteful little girls, do you know that?"

"I don't feel guilty. I—I don't want the baby to suffer

88

. . . well, I don't want anyone to suffer—but I have to get you away from here. You *must* know that I'm afraid of you—"

"*You're* afraid of *us?*"

"You must know I am. You've made me dream things—or maybe it wasn't you—maybe it was the old woman—"

"So it is your dream, is it?"

"What do you mean?"

"We don't dream a thing that comes in the night and frightens our children—why would we?" He shook the little boy off his wrist and shooed him away as if he were a gnat. The little boy stuck his arms out and screeched away, a jet taking off.

"Well, I know I actually dreamt it," said Jen, feeling the old, primitive fear building up from the bottom of her stomach, "but only because you made me."

He stooped a little, to bring his face closer. "Why? Why should we do that?"

She didn't know. She clenched her fists at her sides, the gloves mercifully blanketing her own sharp nails.

"You've come to destroy me," she said, and heard her own voice beginning to sound odd, "because I'm part—traveller—and because I won't have anything to do with that part of me."

He straightened up and laughed. "You are *no* part traveller," he said. It was an insult.

"I *am*. My father—he was a gypsy."

Still he laughed contemptuously.

"Why don't you believe me? It's true. You must know it. Why else would the dreams start just as you came here?"

He reached out his large hands and took her by the

shoulders, gripping hard. "*Your* dream," he said slowly, "is born of *your* venom. It has nothing to do with us—or hadn't, until you set it loose. . . ."

Jen half thought the strange cry came from somewhere else—then knew as she twisted free of his grip that it was hers—turned and ran—avoiding obstacles she didn't focus on—heading for the underpass—panicking the goats who surged together at the full stretch of their ropes—down through the underpass with her footsteps shouting back at her from the walls—up the slope to the pavement and into the bright light—crying and running for home to take up all the offers of comfort she had shrugged away before—to give her nightmare to her mother and let her reduce it to nothing, as mothers can.

# 12

"THEY HAVE POWERS, don't they? And I have their blood!" Jen stood, leaning against the cooker, because she couldn't sit until she had heard what she needed to hear, that she was making a fuss about nothing, and about a situation which existed only in her own mind.

Her mother sat at the kitchen table and looked across the small room and out of the window. She had sat like that, without moving, while Jen told her the whole story, and now she sat on, wearing no expression at all.

Jen waited. Then, "You will help me, won't you?" she said, experiencing doubt for the very first time.

Her mother turned her head and looked across at her. "Where is this—thing—when it isn't apparent?" she said. "When it isn't attacking the camp or following you?"

Jen moved quickly across to the table and leant on it, sat at it, faced her mother. "It isn't *real*," she said urgently. "Don't talk as if it's *real*."

Her mother watched her as if she was watching something very far away and unfamiliar. "You've told me you made it real," she said. "It must be real if it can scratch things—beat in the side of a trailer—"

"People could have done those things," said Jen.

91

"Those scratches could have been there before and I mightn't have noticed them."

Her mother looked at her and said nothing.

Jen put her hands on the table and rested her forehead on them. Because it was real. Her mother knew it was real and that left no more hope of doubt. "What am I going to do?" she said.

"I don't know," said her mother. Then, "I think you'd better go and talk to the old woman, at the encampment."

Jen raised her face. "I can't go to her! I can't go back there!"

"I don't know what else to suggest," said her mother. "She may know what to do."

Jen reached out to touch her mother's hand, and then drew back. "You really think I've done this?" she said.

"It does seem like it. It's said they have powers—I don't know if they have or not, but it's said. And you do have their blood. We need help, and I can't think of anywhere else we could go—with a thing like this. If you like, I'll come with you."

Jen stared at her and then turned and sat sideways in her chair, looking at the wall. It had not, until that moment, occurred to her that her mother might not come with her.

"Not if you don't want me to," said her mother hastily, sensing that her words had jarred.

"I'd like you to come," said Jen quietly, "if you don't mind."

"All right. I'll have to go to the shop, first, to tell Diana I'll be late."

They didn't talk to each other on the way to the boutique. There didn't seem to be anything to say. Jen waited outside, two or three doors down. She didn't want to

hear her mother's excuse, or be drawn into a conversation with Diana.

Later they walked back the way they had come, still
not talking, and took Jen's school route as far as the
flyover. "Will you write me a note?" said Jen, remembering. "For being late."

"Yes."

It was odd to lean on the pedestrian barrier with her
mother. It didn't help the confusion of feelings.

Jen watched the busy rush hour traffic and kept her
eyes averted from the trailers.

"I can see her from here," said her mother, from beside
her.

"I can't go," said Jen, and her teeth were clenched
because her throat felt swollen and she thought she might
be going to retch.

"Do you want me to talk to her first?"

Jen turned her back on the encampment and the traffic
and leant against the barrier. "Are any of the others
there?" she said, not looking.

"There are some kids playing at the other end. I can't
see anyone else. Just the goats—and her, sitting on her
trailer step."

"I'm a coward," said Jen.

"If you want me with you," said her mother, "we've
got to go *now*. This way is like going into a cold sea one
inch at a time."

"That's what I always do," said Jen, her back still
turned towards the camp.

"Yes. Well, it's not what I do." Her mother turned her
back on the barrier and hitched herself up on to it so that
she was sitting beside Jen. But only for a second. All in
one movement she swung her legs over the bar, dropped

93

down on the other side and ran for the huge green island, dodging through the traffic so quickly that, although they blared their horns, not one of the cars had to change speed or direction.

Jen turned to the rancid underpass and ran through it for the second time that morning. She emerged to find her mother waiting for her, breathless, by the goats. She was scratching the head of the nearest one, which was allowing the familiarity with evident pleasure.

Jen strode forward and took her by the arm. "That was *stupid!*" she said angrily.

"Yes."

"You could have been killed. You could have caused a crash. What would you have said if I'd done that?"

"I'm sorry," said her mother quietly. "It isn't as easy as I thought for me to come here. I couldn't stand and think about it any longer." She turned and walked along the line of trailers towards the old woman.

Jen stood where she was. The playing children ignored her. One dog barked twice, but without dedication. She had seen it quiet like this before. She didn't know whether it was that people went out, away from the encampment, or that they shut themselves invisibly in their trailers. And then, probably because she had seen them looking out of their windows that morning, she felt that there were eyes upon her, hostile eyes, watching, and waiting to see what she would do.

In the distance her mother sat on the step beside the old woman, dark hair falling to one side as she turned her head in earnest conversation. The old woman raised her hand regularly to her mouth. There was a faint drift of smoke beside her head. Impossible to see if she spoke, too, or only listened.

She couldn't leave this place, now that her mother was talking with the old woman, but she couldn't make herself join them, either. So she stood still, where she was, somehow feeling that she was the centre of attention, dreading to see the tall gypsy come out of his trailer.

Gradually she made herself look along the windows, one by one. No face looked back at her, no curtain twitched. Even the one vigilant dog had settled down to scratch, face pointing to the sky, lips drawn tight in ecstasy, hind foot kicking away at some nest of fleas. Traffic roared above and beside, enclosing the site in a steady rush of sound, somehow shutting it off from the rest of the world.

She remembered another time when she had felt cut off from reality and the centre of hostile attention, even though she was in no one's sight. She looked quickly all around the encampment. But there were no dark places for any thing to hide in. . . . And anyhow why, if she had made it and sent it to harry them, should it threaten her—why should it have followed her all down those dark streets and seeped into the Welshs' house after her? Why should it seem invisibly present now? If it was her creature, the one compensation for having given birth to it should be that it would protect her—but instead it watched her, and its eye was not friendly.

Her mother stood up on the step of the trailer and signed to Jen to join them. The old woman turned her head impassively towards her. She was too far away for her expression to be visible.

Jen stood, feeling stupid, uneasy about standing still, uneasy about moving forward.

Her mother signed again. Impatiently. She had made her effort. It was Jen's turn.

95

Jen walked across the rough ground to the steps of the small caravan.

"Oh it's you, is it?" said the old woman, leaning forward to peer into Jen's face. "You've been here before, talking with my son. Full of hate, he said. Yet you saved the little dog—I wonder why you bothered?"

"I like animals," said Jen, very conscious of her mother watching her.

"Ah. But not people?"

Jen stood and half looked at them, half let her eyes wander around the site. She said nothing. Sitting on the step, they were both higher than she was, as if they sat in judgement on her. There was nowhere for her to sit unless she wanted to sit on a lower step, at their feet. But she didn't.

"Tell me what your dream is like," said the old woman. The pipe lay neglected on the step beside her, giving out a faint stale smell. She wore so many cardigans and skirts that she looked like a bundle of clothes with a head on top and boots below. But her weather-beaten face was alert and her eyes, although obviously short-sighted, were clear and unclouded.

Jen glanced at her mother, who sat with her arms clasped around her knees, huddled small against the still, cold air. Her nose was pink and she looked unhappy.

"I don't know exactly," said Jen carefully. "It's never very clear. It's something big, but I'm not sure how big. It's got scales. It's long. It's got a kind of sharp point—the sharpness is the thing I'm most sure of—it's got a lot of legs. That's all. It seems—dangerous."

The old woman nodded her head. She had no teeth and when she listened she folded her lips up like cloth.

"The scorpion," she said. "It is dangerous. It's deadly.

96

That's what they half see in the night—the children."

Jen felt as if her bones were shaking. They didn't help, these people, her mother and the old woman, they didn't take it away, they just confirmed it.

Her mother leant forward and put her hand on the woolly arm beside her. The old woman turned her head.

"Is it dangerous to *her,*" said Jen's mother, "or just to you?"

"Of course it's dangerous to her," said the old woman snappishly. "Self-destruction is the surest and cruellest of all."

"So it *is* looking for me—as well as for you—?" said Jen.

"It has looked. It knows where you are now," said the old woman, with a kind of malicious glee. "Oh, it knows all right."

Her eyes darted about, taking in every inch of Jen's face, obviously delighted with what they saw. She's punishing me, Jen thought. She knows every bad thought I've ever had about them. I won't give her the satisfaction of showing that I mind. Aloud she said, "Very well, then, tell me what I can do about it."

"What do you want to do?"

"I want to stop it. I don't want to hurt anyone—I don't want the children frightened. I never meant anything like this to happen. Can it be killed? What do I do?"

Her mother got up from her position on the steps and came slowly down to Jen's level. She linked her arm through Jen's and the two stood side by side and faced the old woman. Who said, "Don't feed it. That's all. Don't feed it and it will fade."

"What does it eat?"

"Oh, *you* know full well what it eats! You've let

it gorge itself on its favourite food—that's why it's so big."

"It really is me, then?" said Jen. "It isn't a dream you sent, like I thought."

"It really is you," said the old woman.

"You can help her more than that if you want to," said Jen's mother.

"Help her? I've seen too many like her. They want to buy heather, and buy their fortunes, and buy a piece of luck, and buy a piece of advice, and pay to keep off the ill-wishing—and when that's all over and done with they want to destroy us."

"She's not like those people," said her mother. "It's all got confused inside, that's all. It isn't always easy to be a traveller, I know that, but it isn't easy to be half of something, either."

"She's confused, you're saying," said the old woman, and her voice was a little higher and faster than before. "And *we* have to suffer the consequences of her confusion."

"I don't want anyone to suffer!" said Jen. "I saw the little baby—" The pressure of her mother's arm and the thought of the baby were suddenly too much and the tears began. "I don't want to make him suffer. Help me not make him suffer."

"He needs a lot of things," said the old woman tersely, "but not a raincloud of tears. Give him rheumatism."

"Listen," said Jen's mother. "I know some of you have powers, perhaps all of you. I know *you* do. Help her for her father's sake if not for hers or mine."

The little, bright black eyes flickered from one to the other of their faces. The old woman relaxed slightly, as if revenge had been sweet but she had had enough for now.

She held out a pair of claw-like hands. "Here," she said. Without a word Jen disengaged her arm from her mother and held out her own hands. The old woman took them between hers and closed her eyes.

Jen stood, leaning uncomfortably forward, one knee on a step, looking at the brown marks on the backs of the hands that held hers.

And all at once the old woman began to shake. At first Jen thought it was with emotion—then she saw it was with laughter. She opened her eyes, such bright little black eyes, and looked at Jen, still laughing. Then she turned to the girl beside Jen and spoke to her, as if Jen wasn't there at all.

"It isn't the 'gypsy' part of her that's dreamt this thing," she said. "It's the Gorgio part. There's nothing I can do about it." And went on laughing, cackling wheezily to herself.

# 13

It didn't come for three nights; and when it did she didn't know at first that it was a dream because she was in her own small room, in her own narrow bed, the furniture dimly visible in the sparse light that came through from the street. She lay there, looking across at the wall, and she felt as she had felt before, that she was being watched. Attention was upon her.

She wanted to look out of the window because she knew that it was outside, but her body felt leaden and she couldn't make it sit up to draw back the curtains. Couldn't even open her eyes. That was when she knew she must be dreaming because although she could see her room her eyes were closed.

She began to try to wake herself up. She tried first to make a movement, thinking that would break the spell, and then to make a sound. But it was not possible.

She lay there, heavy and inert, and was all at once vividly aware of the outside of the building—of the great expanse of brickwork, interlocked like scales, and of the hard, sharp, black spikes on top of the railings that grew from the ground. Her awareness stretched further, to the flyover with its long, undulating shape and its dozens of legs, set in pairs; to the scene below the flyover where people whose existence she didn't begin to understand had made a pattern of their lives and belongings, a design in flesh and metal, their bodies protected by the hard outer shell of the trailers.

And then she seemed to be sitting up in bed, sketching in the long, threatening shape of the scorpion, raising her pencil and bringing it down with precision to dig its sharp point in to the paper in a mark which suggested an eye. And the eye, the small black dot, grew. And she looked into it, fascinated, but it was just blackness which grew and absorbed her until she felt that she only existed as a reflection in this monstrous eye.

And then it was in her room, with her, but it was not exactly her room because there seemed to be limitless space for this thing to move in, and it was huge, monstrous, out of all proportion.

Before she had time to be seriously afraid she realised with relief that it hadn't noticed her; it was rearing up with its front half and bending its primitive head downwards to threaten a figure which stood in front of it. This figure was of a big, swarthy man, with black greasy hair and thick dirty arms appearing below the rolled up sleeves of his shirt. At first the man stood his ground with a kind of brutish courage although he was clearly very afraid, partly looking up into the faceless face and partly looking higher at the vicious sting which now arched above the armoured head.

Jen was too afraid for herself to try to help in any way, but then the man began to back away from the creature and as he moved his outline began to flow about and waver, like oil on water, and to reshape itself. And as he drew further from the shadow of the thing Jen saw that he was not the hefty ruffian he had appeared to be, he was not big at all, it was a trick of the light, he was young and slightly built.

He raised his arm to ward off the imminent blow, a slim fair boy looking up at the lethal sting as it drew back to strike.

"No!" Jen screamed, but heard footsteps, running, before the sound was half out of her mouth, and a woman came from behind the creature, running along its length. The ancient, cruel head creaked round to regard her, and turned to follow her as she ran round in front of it. Jen's attention, and the scorpion's, had been distracted, neither had seen where her father had escaped to, but he was no longer there and in his place was a middle-aged, dumpy woman, her hair in a bun, her whole front covered by a serviceable white apron which reached to the ground.

"Get her instead," Jen called, crouching in her bed, the pillow held in front of her.

The creature moved its head from side to side as if lining the woman up in its vision and then stabbed forwards with the spike on its tail, over its head and down in a movement so fast that Jen never saw the blow struck, just saw the woman fall on to her side and begin to curl up like an embryo. Again the creature struck, and again, and with each cut the woman was pushed further across the floor. She turned on to her hands and knees and began to crawl away, her dark hair loose now, trying to stand but always falling forward on to her hands again. The vicious blows rained down on to her narrow shoulders, but still she kept going, a slimmer and more delicate figure than she had seemed at first. And all at once she turned her head as if to meet the final blow head on and the face was clearly visible to Jen. It was her mother. She was desperately afraid, she was crying, but she was in control, her expression without hope, yet her eyes alert for a way out.

"No, no, no!" Jen screamed. "No! Not her! Leave them! It's me!"

Tears coursed down her face and she stood up on the bed. The fear had dissolved into a deep pool of sadness which was spilling out of her, yet still full.

She was alone in the room with the sharpness and the scales. She was the pupil of its eye.

The ancient, mindless face turned, slowly, and bent towards her. The narrow end of the scaly body arched again, upwards and over the head, and as it moved it creaked like dungeon doors. The sting appeared over the brow and pointed so directly at the centre of her vision that she could hardly see it. It shone. It was hard, sharp, but not just sharp, full of poison. Shooting pains rose up to greet it from every area of her body.

"You are nothing," she said into the primeval face. "I have no more food for you. There is nothing in me to keep you alive."

It was somehow transparent, she saw, though not clear; transparent like smoke, vapour. The tension in its form seemed to relax, the curved tail sank down until the sting rested on the floor, and it lowered the fore part of its body until it stood along the ground, still facing her.

"You don't exist," Jen sobbed. "You should never have existed."

It had no eyes, this thing, which gave it an odd, blunt look. It lay along the floor like a cloud and there was no kind of expression on its primitive face—indeed, its face had no facilities for expression. Gaps began to appear down its length, as gaps of blue sky show through when a cloud formation is breaking up.

There was just a vague, patchy suggestion of something scaly, of a sharpness. Then the scaly mist evaporated and the sharp, vicious spike went out—as a flame goes out—ceasing to be.

Jen woke up in her empty bedroom, her head resting on a pillow sodden with tears.

* * * * * *

They had been standing leaning on the pedestrian barrier for nearly an hour, she and her mother, watching as the travellers struck camp and hitched the vehicles up to the trailers. No one looked across at them and they made no attempt to go any nearer.

"Someone else," said her mother, "would have seen to it that they were moved on if you hadn't."

"Yes," said Jen.

"I don't think you should really stay away from school any longer. They'll start asking me for a doctor's certificate or something."

The first of the trailers, towed by the clapped-out old truck, moved across the site and bumped down on to the road. It turned its back on them and moved off under the flyover and away. The next trailer was already bumping on to the road, and the engine of every vehicle seemed to be running.

Jen held on to the top rail of the barrier. "I only did it because I was afraid of them," she said.

"It usually is fear," said her mother.

"And also I thought—Tom—would—think better of me if I proved I wasn't them."

"Will you go in to school this morning?" said her mother quietly.

The last trailer pulled off the site and turned slowly away. Jen felt a dragging feeling in her stomach as if the tide was going out and she could feel the pull of the retreating water.

"I should have gone and talked to them," she said.

"Better not," said her mother, "now. Some other day—other people—there'll always be others."

"I'll go to school tomorrow," said Jen.

"All right."

They were completely out of sight, now, but still she stared, with a feeling almost of panic as she realised that there was no way to call them back, no sure way to find them ever again.

Her mother turned away from the barrier. "Tom's coming down the road," she said. "Perhaps you could go to school with him?"

Jen looked quickly at the approaching figure and then away. "I wrote him a note," she said. "I tried to explain . . ."

She watched her feet, seeing her shoes more vividly than she had in all her life—every little crease in the leather, every tiny scuff mark. His shadow fell across her feet and she looked up.

"Hallo," said her mother.

"Hallo," said Tom, not looking at Jen.

"Hallo," said Jen. Tom said nothing, seemed to think that Jen's mother stood alone on the pavement, turned and went on his way.

Everything gone. The site cleared and starkly empty. Tom's retreating figure growing smaller.

Her mother touched her arm gently. "Let's go home, eh?" she said.

# THE SECRET LINE
William Corlett

Neither black nor white, Jo Carson feels ill at ease in her skin. But then Mit, a longlost childhood friend appears and takes her to the Secret Line – a mysterious section of the Underground with stations such as Heath, where she meets the engaging runaway David. But further down the line, at Jungle, danger lurks in the shape of the vicious thug Straker...

"Most interesting and most ambitious."
*The Observer*

# THE FIRST TIME
## Aisling Foster

It's the summer term at William Stubbs Comp-
rehensive and romance is in the air. Not for
Rosa, though – style and painting are the loves of
her life. But, as Rosa's sex maniac mum keeps
telling her, there's a first time for everything. The
important thing is to get it right...

"Brilliant and affectionate style-wars novel."
*The Sunday Telegraph*

# MORE WALKER PAPERBACKS

## For You to Enjoy